The New York Times

CHANGING PERSPECTIVES

The Death Penalty

EDUCATIONAL PUBLISHING BOOKS

THE NEW YORK TIMES EDITORIAL STAFF

Published in 2020 by The New York Times Educational Publishing in association with The Rosen Publishing Group, Inc.
29 East 21st Street, New York, NY 10010

First Edition

The New York Times
Alex Ward: Editorial Director, Book Development
Phyllis Collazo: Photo Rights/Permissions Editor
Heidi Giovine: Administrative Manager

Rosen Publishing
Megan Kellerman: Managing Editor
Jacob R. Steinberg: Editor
Greg Tucker: Creative Director
Brian Garvey: Art Director

Cataloging-in-Publication Data
Names: New York Times Company.
Title: The death penalty / edited by the New York Times editorial staff.
Description: New York : New York Times Educational Publishing, 2020. | Series: Changing perspectives | Includes glossary and index.
Identifiers: ISBN 9781642822243 (library bound) | ISBN 9781642822236 (pbk.) | ISBN 9781642822250 (ebook)
Subjects: LCSH: Capital punishment—United States—Juvenile literature. | Capital punishment—Juvenile literature.
Classification: LCC HV8699.U5 D343 2020 |
DDC 364.660973—dc23

Manufactured in the United States of America

On the cover: A view of the death chamber from the witness room at the Southern Ohio Correctional Facility in Lucasville, Ohio, Aug. 29, 2001; Mike Simons/Stringer/Getty Images.

Contents

CHAPTER 3

From Furman to Gregg, a Brief Moratorium on Executions

CHAPTER 4

Intellectual Disability and the Death Penalty

CHAPTER 7

Medical Perspectives

CHAPTER 8

Perspectives From the Bench

CHAPTER 9

Lethal Injection and the Death Penalty Today

Introduction

WHILE IN INTERNATIONAL forums the United States often revels in its identity as the standard-bearer for democracy and human rights, there is one practice that it continues to engage in that places it in the uneasy company of the likes of China, Iran and Saudi Arabia, among other flagrant violators of human rights. That practice is its continued use of the death penalty.

Whereas the majority of the Western world has gradually eschewed the practice over the last century or so, the United States has ignored calls from international bodies and humanitarian groups to abandon the death penalty. In fact, certain states persist in rewriting their statutes to pass the continually higher bar set by the courts for when and how the death penalty may be applied.

This disparity between begs the questions: Why is the death penalty so entrenched in the American legal system? Why do a majority of Americans (as shown by popular opinion polls) continue to support a practice found barbaric by most of their allies abroad? The answers aren't so simple.

Capital punishment has always been part of the American criminal justice system. In colonial times, the American system of law was derived from the English penal code and bore religious tinges. Infractions that today seem minor warranted an execution in some colonies, including the crimes of denying God, cursing a parent, stealing grapes or trading with Native Americans.

Not all colonies, however, were quite as bloodthirsty as others. Notably, areas with Quaker influence, such as Pennsylvania and West Jersey, limited the use of capital punishment to cases of treason or murder.

YAREK WASZUL

The courts have become the main arena for advocates and opponents of the death penalty. Cases reviewed by the Supreme Court have faced particular public scrutiny.

By the late 1700s, a true abolitionist movement had begun to form in the United States. One prominent abolitionist was Dr. Benjamin Rush, a signer of the Declaration of Independence, who called the death penalty "un-Christian" and challenged its deterrent effect. Several states limited the list of crimes for which offenders could be sentenced to death, and further, some prohibited public hangings.

Throughout the 1800s, many states abolished the practice only to later reinstate it, and an abolitionist wave between 1907 and 1917 came to a halt as public fervor again prompted its return in several of the states that had banned it.

Since the 1960s, the greatest challenge to capital punishment has not come from the legislatures, but the courts. The N.A.A.C.P. Legal Defense and Educational Fund adopted a successful strategy of challenging the practice in courts on grounds that it violated the Eighth Amendment's protection from "cruel and unusual punishment."

The cruxes of such legal challenges have varied from focus on the inconsistent application of the death penalty to different types of defendants — often influenced by racial prejudice — to legitimate concerns over the painlessness and effectiveness of different means of execution. Because of such challenges, the death penalty's application has been greatly limited.

While a unidirectional historical trajectory can be plotted for many social issues, the death penalty has seen waves of support and challenges. As courts further curb its use in response to evolving standards of decency, legislatures concoct new standards of application that they hope will pass muster when legally challenged. And much like in the colonial era, support and rejection of capital punishment varies greatly by state. Indeed, just a handful of states — among them Texas, Virginia, Oklahoma and Florida — execute a disproportionately high number of offenders compared with the rest of the country.

The articles that follow explore the many diverse perspectives on a heated topic, taking into account religious, medical and legal perspectives on what is literally a matter of life and death.

CHAPTER 1

The Ultimate Punishment, but Is It a Deterrent?

One of the strongest arguments for maintaining the death penalty has been that it is a deterrent to crime. Its supporters believe fear of capital punishment causes would-be criminals to think twice before committing a violent offense. Detractors argue that its inconsistent application in different states and to different types of defendants nullifies that argument. The following articles focus on the death penalty's ability — or failure — to prevent crime.

Is the Death Penalty an Actual Check to Crime?

BY THE NEW YORK TIMES | MAY 16, 1909

Dr. Edward C. Spitzka gives the results of recent investigations.

THAT THE ABOLITION or practical abrogation of the death penalty in European countries has made unsafe the lives of the sovereigns of those countries and has made it dangerous for other rulers to visit them — such is one of the conclusions which seem inevitable after a conversation with Dr. Edward C. Spitzka, the noted New York alienist, who has made a special study of these subjects.

Another is that by the abolition of the death penalty in these countries it has been demonstrated — what it has been impossible to demonstrate hitherto — that capital punishment does deter criminals from crime in greater degree than does imprisonment.

Another is that the reformation of such a criminal by a life in prison is an iridescent dream.

In talking of his researches, Dr. Spitzka explains that for purposes of a fair comparison it is necessary to take a group of murderers of the same class, and most of his illustrations, therefore, are drawn from regicides and Anarchists.

"There are a number of cases already, on record," he said to a Sunday Times reporter yesterday, "where men who had served a sentence for a felonious murder — not all murders are felonious — shortly after release from prison committed a second murder, also from felonious motives.

> *Two of these cases deserve special mention because of the prominence of the victim, and also because they prove that a mistaken humanitarian policy coddles and preserves a criminal who has really forfeited his right to life, in order to set him free to destroy those of law-abiding citizens. By doing so it tenders itself practically guilty of accessoryship before the fact of the second crime. The conservative policy would have sacrificed the life of an undesirable citizen and preserved the lives of useful members of the community, who were really entitled to its protection.*
>
> *The first instance is that of the murder of the Greek Prime Minister Delyannis, who was killed in a particularly treacherous way. He was leaving the Chamber of Deputies and about to enter his carriage, when a man named Ghekaris opened the carriage door for him to enter, and while he was bowing in acknowledgment of the courtesy the man stabbed him to death.*
>
> *The criminal had served a term of imprisonment for the murder of his wife. What reformative influence the prison had exerted upon him may be judged from the motive of his second crime, which was resentment at the Minister's proceeding against the gambling hells of Athens, in one of which the murderer was interested.*
>
> *The second one occurred in Leghorn, Italy. The editor of a daily paper was stabbed to death by a certain Lucchesi as he was leaving his carriage. Shortly before this Lucchesi had been discharged from prison,*

where he had served a long term for another murder. It was on his trial for this first crime that his counsel had utilized in his defense the Lombroso degeneracy doctrine.

Bandi, the editor, had written an editorial stigmatizing this procedure as a dodge in that particular case, and denouncing the Lombroso theory as an unfounded one in general. This article was so convincingly written that the prosecutor waived making an argument, and instead read the editorial to the jury, which promptly convicted the prisoner. The latter utilized the reforming atmosphere of the prison to feed his grudge and keep it warm, and satiated his vengeance against the man who, as he thought, was the cause of his conviction, by the second murder. The excuse he gave, however, was that he had killed Bandi to avenge Santos, the assassin of the French President Carnot — Bandi having written an editorial deploring that crime.

The opponents of capital punishment have really furnished its advocates with a conclusive argument in favor of the death penalty. In the past one of the disadvantages under which the conservatives stood was their inability to meet the enormous material of exemplifications of the death penalty's failure to deter from crime — every capital crime being an argument against the theory of deterrence — by equally concrete proof of its positive deterrent action.

The conservatives could only refer in a general way to that large number of persons who did not commit the crime as being deterred by the death penalty, but that was hypothetical and dealing with a quantity of unknown dimensions. But this is a desideratum no longer. By abolishing capital punishment in some parts of Europe there was furnished an opportunity for a differential test, and the Anarchists who acted in both territories are the test — that is, they furnish the test material.

Of thirty-two plots against the lives of European sovereigns since 1894, twenty-five transpired in the death penalty territory and seven in countries where capital punishment had been abolished. Here is an analysis of these thirty-two plots.

DEATH PENALTY TERRITORY

- Of twenty-five plots, five, or one-fifth, resulted in attacks.
- All were fiascos.

• The only weapon used was a bomb.

• Not one assailant was captured on the spot, and only two of them brought to bay at all.

• In thirteen plots, those concerned maintained the incognito or betrayed their plot to the Government in order to escape the alternative which threatened them if they carried it out on the one hand, and the renegade's fate if they refused, on the other.

NO DEATH PENALTY

• Of seven plots, six resulted in attacks.

• Two succeeded.

• Steel and revolver used exclusively.

• All faced capture on the spot.

• Practically nothing occurred of this kind.

Dr. Spitzka took the view that this showing indicated the paralyzing or fear-provoking effect of the knowledge that capital punishment awaited the plotter. Of especial significance, in his opinion, was the use of the bomb, which he called "the coward's weapon" — partially exempting Russian political assassins from this characterization, however. When steel or revolver is used, the assassin has comparatively little chance of escaping, and so has his victim.

"Had the twenty-five of the first group," said Dr. Spitzka, "selected the same weapons and used them with the same determination as the seven of the other, the presumable result would have been not five but twenty attacks; not stereotyped failure, but six or seven regicidal tragedies. That, instead of throwing nations into mourning, the twenty-five attempts excited their derision, was due to the selection of a weapon which, as a critical analysis of the entire field shows, is proof presumptive of pusillanimous self-solicitude.

And as their fear of the scaffold coerced them to this choice and determined their failure, it is entitled to the credit of having defeated the criminal purpose of a quarter of a hundred plots, either by causing the stage fright of the contemplator or by paralyzing the energy and courage of the perpetrator of regicide. For in every other respect than the penal contingency, the twenty-five and the seven were as nearly identical in condition as is conceivable.

They were all racially akin, of the same social class, all acted in the interest of the same cause, in the same enterprise, against the same class of victims — the highest. The only difference was that one set acted within the shadow of the threatened scaffold, and the other in countries where the life of the chief of State or his traveling royal guest is less secure than that of their assassin.

It has been claimed that the Anarchists, instead of being deterred by the death penalty, are actually seduced to their crime by the prospect of notoriety and martyr glory on the scaffold. The evidence shows that whatever the attractive power of this magnet is, it does not endow the assassins with any formidable energy. For all the successful Anarchists since 1894 in Europe were in the territory where there is no death penalty to fear, and not once has it happened that the ruler of a country where capital punishment has been abolished was attacked on the territory where it is still enforced.

But the contrary has happened twice. In one case with fatal results. That was when an Italian residing in France traveled to a Swiss canton in which the death penalty had been abolished to kill the Empress of Austria.

In the other case an Italian named Sipido, residing in France, traveled to Brussels to attack the heir apparent of England, who passed through that city. In Belgium the death penalty had been in disuse for fifty years. Rubino, who shot at the King of Belgium himself, blundered into the admission that he had a choice of sovereigns to attack.

As the event shows, he seems not to have been attracted by the prospect of martyr glory, which would have been easily achieved in France or Germany or England, but preferred precisely the little territory of Belgium, where his life was safe.

A fourth Anarchist owed the discovery of his plot to his procrastinating his attack, which was to have taken place in Marseilles, to a less perilous region where the death penalty is abolished — to Rome, which city the French President Loubet was announced to visit.

The man from whose case this talk of the attraction of the scaffold and martyr glory is traced — Reinsdorf — himself denied his guilt and attempted to escape the glory on two trials. At the dedication of the colossal statue of Germania in 1883, Reinsdorf had constructed under the railroad tracks a mine which, if it had been exploded, would have destroyed all the great Generals and intellectual leaders of Germany at one blow.

Reinsdorf did not himself go to the scene of the intended crime, but sent a young fellow named Rupsch, a young enthusiast; but he did not trust the mere enthusiasm of Rupsch, and sent a man named Kuchler to watch and see that the work was properly done. As soon as the rattle of the train over the viaduct was heard, Rupsch was to ignite a time fuse with his cigar.

In his confession Rupsch said that as the train came along he was seized for the first time with such a sudden realization of the tremendous import of his act that he, to deceive Kuchler, touched the fuse wlth the mouth end of his cigar instead of the lighted end. Thus he saved all those lives. The fact is that Kuchler himself was so dazed that he did not have his eyes open.

The three were at length suspected, and were placed under arrest. The first examination was without result. Reinsdorf's stereotyped answer to every question was, "I know nothing about it; I have nothing to say." The authorities felt pretty sure of their guilt, and discharged them, as a ruse, allowing them to come together under a surveillance unknown to them. On this occasion Reinsdorf did not differ at all from his colleagues in expressing dismay at the narrowness of their escape and wonder how the Government could have guessed so correctly the identity of the plotters.

Rupsch was laid hold of first, and he blundered into so many things that afforded the Government clues that the men were indicted. On the real trial Reinsdorf resorted to every technicality that could afford any chance of escape. It was not until every possibility of acquittal had been destroyed by Rupsch's admissions that Reinsdorf suddenly changed his attitude and posed theatrically as a martyr and a hero.

To give the devil his due, Reinsdorf died like a man, but Kuchler presented the worst picture of utter, desperate breakdown that has ever been recorded of any victim of the block and axe. In an attempt to save his life he had even changed from an Anarchist to a Roman Catholic. As for Reinsdorf, he was a consumptive, and said he regarded the Government as saving him the pain of a lingering death — as administering to him euthanasia.

The Death Penalty

EDITORIAL | BY THE NEW YORK TIMES | MARCH 3, 1910

THE SUPPORTERS OF a bill to restore the death penalty in Rhode Island, which has done without it since 1852, present figures of curious interest. The State of Maine, also, has abolished capital punishment, and it is found that in the census year 1900 homicides in Maine were almost twice as many per 100,000 population as in Massachusetts, which retains the penalty; twice Connecticut's, four and a half times as many homicides as New Hampshire's, and twice as many as Vermont's. Rhode Island had two and a half times as many as Massachusetts, three times Connecticut's, three times Vermont's, and six and a half times as many as New Hampshire. These statistics are sufficient to alarm the Mayor of Providence, three Police Commissioners, and the city's Chief of Police.

But, as The Springfield Republican ably points out, the figures prove nothing at all with respect to the effectiveness or non-effectiveness of the death penalty. They show in certain cases as violent discrepancies between the numbers of homicides in Vermont, Connecticut, Massachusetts, and New Hampshire, States where the death penalty was inflicted in 1900, as between them and the two States which dispensed with capital punishment. The homicides of only one year are chosen as the basis of comparison, which is, of course, too narrow a basis. But even statistics for half a century could not be correctly interpreted without reference to the different social and environmental conditions of the New England States. Moreover, the death penalty is not especially deterrent. England of two centuries ago, when forty different crimes and misdemeanors were punishable by death, was more desperately criminal than any modern American State. And here and now the legal taking of life is regarded with such horror that juries are prone to let murderers go scot free rather than convict them. Perhaps the law is better enforced under Rhode Island's less barbarous penalties.

Panel Urges End to Death Penalty; Psychiatrists Told That It Fails as a Deterrent

BY THE NEW YORK TIMES | MAY 15, 1966

ATLANTIC CITY, MAY 14 — A former Governor, a social philosopher and a psychiatrist this week urged the medical and legal profession to unite in a campaign for the abolition of the death penalty.

They called capital punishment a failure as a deterrent to crime, a soporific to demands for penal and social reform and an incentive to warped mentalities for whom murder is close to suicide.

The indictment and the call for action were issued by a panel addressing a meeting at the 122nd annual convention of the American Psychiatric Association, which ended yesterday.

Nearly 4,000 psychiatrists and 2,000 guests attended the five days of meetings at Convention Hall.

The panel included Michael V. DiSalle, former Governor of Ohio; Dr. Hugo A. Bedau, visiting professor of philosophy at Princeton University, and Dr. Louis J. West, head of the Department of Psychiatry, Neurology and Behavioral Sciences at the University of Oklahoma School of Medicine.

POLLS ARE CITED

They noted that while polls showed no more than 45 per cent of Americans supporting capital punishment, it was retained by 37 states and the Federal Government.

And although only seven executions were carried out last year, the number of prisoners under sentence of death is increasing, with more than 200 awaiting execution in 1965, Dr. Bedau said.

Dr. Bedau said that "there is no scientific evidence that the death penalty is a superior deterrent to crimes of personal violence than is some form of imprisonment, or even that it is a deterrent at all."

Mr. DiSalle said the death penalty was "used more in vengeance than in protection and provided an excuse for not getting to work on the true needs of society."

Dr. West agreed, adding that the death penalty led to a false sense of security that gave "the illusion of safety engendered by the death penalty's false promise."

'LEGAL EXTERMINATION'

Noting that the death penalty had been abolished in most of the Western democracies but not in Communist countries or in the United States, Dr. West declared:

> *Legal extermination of human beings in any society generates a profound tendency among the citizens to accept killing as a solution to human problems.*

More than that, Dr. West said, the death penalty "breeds murder" by catering to the suicide impulse.

He described three cases in which murderers were infuriated because juries either declared them insane and therefore unfit for trial or sentenced them to life imprisonment.

Deadly Statistics: A Survey of Crime and Punishment

BY FORD FESSENDEN | SEPT. 22, 2000

IN ITS ANALYSIS, The New York Times examined homicide rates in two groups of states: the 12 states without the death penalty and the 36 states that passed laws within 10 years of the Supreme Court's 1972 Furman v. Georgia decision, which overturned all existing death penalty statutes. (New York and Kansas did not adopt the death penalty until the 1990's.)

The analysis found that homicide rates have not declined any more in the states that instituted the death penalty than in states that did not.

In fact, year after year, homicide rates in states with death penalties roughly mirrored the rates in states without capital punishment, with death penalty states 48 percent to 101 percent higher. That trend, criminologists say, provides evidence that something besides enactment of capital punishment laws drives homicides.

"It's clear that the states with the death penalty may want it more because they have more homicides," said Alfred Blumstein, director of the National Consortium on Violence Research at Carnegie Mellon University. "But it's not clear that it does them any good in terms of reducing homicide."

Even after executions resumed, homicide rates appeared unaffected, the analysis found. In the 21 states that carried out their first executions by 1993, homicide rates declined a collective 5 percent over the four years after the execution. But rates declined 12 percent in states that had not had executions in the same years.

The Times also looked at contiguous and demographically similar states, and found no pattern that differentiated death penalty states from those without capital punishment. Massachusetts and Rhode Island, with no death penalty, had homicide rates of 3.7 per 100,000 and 4.2 per 100,000, respectively, from 1977 to 1997, while Connecticut, a death penalty state, had a rate of 4.9 per 100,000.

The survey by The Times is similar to the type of analysis criminologists used in the years before the Supreme Court's Furman decision to conclude that state homicide rates were not affected by death penalty laws. The review by The Times confirms that those patterns appear to continue under the new era of capital punishment statutes.

Some researchers still contend that the death penalty has a measurable deterrent effect. "The statistics involved in such comparisons have long been recognized as devoid of scientific merit," Prof. Isaac Ehrlich, of the State University of New York at Buffalo, said of the analysis by The Times. He said that if variations like unemployment, income inequality, likelihood of apprehension and willingness to use the death penalty are accounted for, the death penalty shows a significant deterring effect. Most criminologists, however, discount Professor Ehrlich's work.

CHAPTER 2

A Question of Fairness: Race, Class and the Death Penalty

In recent decades, the most successful challenge to the constitutionality of the death penalty has been the argument that it is inconsistently applied to different defendants. Because of variation in state laws, convicts in one state may face a sentence of capital punishment while those convicted of the same crime elsewhere may not. Further, statistics support the argument that racial minorities and low-income defendants are sentenced to the death penalty in disproportionately higher numbers.

Casting Off a Remnant of Racism

EDITORIAL | BY THE NEW YORK TIMES | JULY 10, 1977

IN ITS LAST ACT before the summer recess, the Supreme Court, in a case entitled Coker v. Georgia, wiped out one of the grosser remnants of racism in the United States. It decided that the death penalty for the rape of an adult constitutes cruel and unusual punishment, in violation of the Eighth Amendment.

Execution for rape had a unique place in the racial history of the United States. It enforced the powerful taboo against sexual relations between black men and white women. Its purpose was plainly exposed when 19th-century Georgia statute provided the death penalty for a black rapist of a white woman but lesser penalties for a white man guilty of the same crime. Although that particular law was thrown out long ago, the courts of this country kept its spirit alive. In the relatively enlightened period since 1930, for example, 455 men were put to death for rape — and 405 of them were black.

That record prompted the Legal Defense Fund of the National Association for the Advancement of Colored People to set out a decade ago to eliminate the death penalty in rape cases. It began by charging that in practice the penalty was discriminatory on racial grounds. Soon, however, the fund found itself engaged in a broader range of cases aimed at eliminating the death penalty altogether.

The effort to strike down all executions is still before the courts; laws have had to be tightened, and at least judges and juries are now required to deliberate much more carefully before they impose a death sentence. Its use in rape cases, however, was not squarely faced until the Coker case. Ironically, the defendant in the case was white, and the Supreme Court never discussed race deciding it. As Jack Greenberg, the fund's director counsel, has often noted, "rights asserted by blacks, when ultimately granted, so often benefit everyone without regard to race."

High Court to Decide Whether Death Penalty Discriminates Against Blacks

BY KENNETH B. NOBLE | MARCH 23, 1987

ATLANTA, MARCH 19 — On the evening of May 13, 1978, four men entered the Dixie Furniture Store here, secured the showroom by forcing everyone to lie face down on the floor, and as they searched for cash, one of them shot and killed a police officer.

Three of the men were sentenced to varying prison terms for the crime, while another, Warren McCleskey, was convicted of murder and sentenced to death.

Like most of those now on Georgia's death row, Mr. McClesky is black, and his victim was white. He is extraordinary only in that his appeal is the first to be heard by the United States Supreme Court based on the contention that Georgia's death-sentencing process is unconstitutionally infected by racial discrimination.

RACE OF VICTIM CALLED CRUCIAL

To accept the full implications of Mr. McClesky's argument, however, the Court, which is expected to rule as soon as this week, might have to throw out the capital sentencing system not only in Georgia, but also in many other states.

Mr. McCleskey's sentence, handed down by a jury of 11 whites and one black, is viewed by opponents of the death penalty as perhaps the last broad-based challenge to the way the death penalty is imposed in most states and the last opportunity to save many of the 1,874 convicts now on death row.

Individual death sentences will continue to be appealed, no matter how the Supreme Court acts on the case. But if the Court decides against Mr. McCleskey, future appellants will essentially be limited to arguing that a miscarriage of justice occurred in their particular cases.

Mr. McCleskey's lawyers argued that blacks who killed whites were by far the most likely convicts to be sentenced to die.

BITTER DISSENT PROVOKED

"Race is the preeminent factor in deciding who lives and who dies in capital punishment cases, particularly here in the death belt states," said Steven B. Bright, an attorney with the Southern Prisoners Defense Committee, which represents indigent capital defendants.

"When you kill the organist at the Methodist church who is white, you're going to get the death penalty, but if you kill the black Baptist organist, the likelihood is that it'll be plea bargained down to a life sentence," Mr. Bright said.

This argument has provoked increasingly bitter dissent from supporters of the death penalty. Daniel J. Popeo, general counsel of the Washington Legal Foundation, a conservative public interest law organization, called Mr. McClesky's case "a concocted effort on the part of the anti-death penalty lobby to block the enforcement of the law."

"If there wasn't this excuse to block the death penalty, they'd manufacture another," Mr. Popeo said. "The bottom line is that they're running out of legal stalling tactics."

ATTACK ON THE SOUTH

The case has also disturbed some civic leaders here, who see it as another in a long history of unwarranted attacks on the South's criminal justice system.

"This part of the country, and Georgia in particular, is certainly not free from taint, but to say that, today, Georgia's criminal justice system is permeated by racial discrimination, is absolutely inaccurate," said Michael Bowers, Georgia's Attorney General.

The appeal by the NAACP Legal Defense and Educational Fund Inc. in McCleskey v. Kemp, is based on both the Eighth Amendment's prohibition against cruel and unusual punishment and the 14th Amendment's guarantee of equal protection.

Mr. McCleskey's argument that his sentence was tainted by racial discrimination is not based on allegations of discriminatory acts by a prosecutor or judge, but on statistics.

Since the Supreme Court first upheld some revised death penalty laws in 1976 after striking down all existing death penalty laws four years earlier, there have been 70 executions: 1 in 1977, 2 in 1979, 1 in 1981, 2 in 1982, 5 in 1983, 21 in 1984, 18 in 1985, 18 in 1986 and 2 so far this year.

NEARLY ALL MURDERED WHITES

Forty-two of those executed, or 60 percent, were black; 26 were white and 2 were Hispanic.

What is more striking, however, than the race of those executed is the race of their victims. Although blacks and whites are the victims of homicide in roughly equal numbers, about 95 percent of those executed since 1977 have been convicted of murdering whites, as were 69 percent of those remaining on death row.

Those figures provide the context for an independent study of the death penalty in Georgia that is at the heart of the case now before the Court. David Baldus, a law professor at the University of Iowa, studied the 2,484 homicides that occurred in Georgia from 1973 to 1979.

In those cases, 1,665 defendants were black and 819 were white. Blacks were the victims of homicides in about 61 percent of the cases, whites in 39 percent.

230 FACTORS IDENTIFIED

The Baldus study did not find that black defendants overall were more likely to get the death sentence than white defendants. But it did find that of the 2,484 murders in Georgia, blacks who had killed whites were sentenced to death at three times the rate of whites who killed blacks.

Professor Baldus identified 230 factors, such as the viciousness of the crime, the quality of the evidence and the defendant's criminal background, that figure in a sentencing determination. He focused on those murders that were neither the most nor the least notorious, the "midrange cases" in which the greatest jury discretion was exercised.

He concluded that in the 128 cases in which a death sentence was imposed, 22 percent of black defendants who had killed whites were sentenced to death, compared to 3 percent of white defendants who had killed blacks, 8 percent of whites who had killed whites and 1 percent of blacks who had killed blacks.

COURT LEERY OF SOCIAL SCIENCE

Still, Mr. McCleskey faces a formidable obstacle in his effort to overturn his conviction based on statistics: the historical reluctance of judges to use social science as a basis for legal precedent in criminal cases. Courts have accepted arguments based on such statistics in cases involving employment and housing discrimination, for example, but the Supreme Court has never applied such analysis to criminal law.

Judge Owen Forrest, a United States district judge who rejected Mr. McCleskey's sociological argument in a 1984 ruling, said: "As a general proposition, the scholarly literature suggests that it is troublesome" to base decisions largely on such statistics "in that the law can be made to change as new studies or new scientific developments come about."

The United States Court of Appeals for the 11th Circuit also rejected Mr. McCleskey's challenge in a 9-to-3 decision in 1985. The court said it assumed the Baldus study to be valid, but held that the data failed as a matter of law to establish a constitutional violation because there was no proof of deliberate racial prejudice by an identifiable source.

In oral arguments last October before the Supreme Court, a lawyer for the state of Georgia hypothesized that the apparent racial disparities could be explained by the generally more aggravated nature of murders with white victims.

AN ALTERNATIVE EXPLANATION

Mary Beth Westmoreland, an assistant Georgia attorney general, said the statistics did not necessarily prove discrimination because blacks were more often killed in "family disputes, lover disputes," bar fights and the like, whereas whites were more often killed in robberies and other situations more likely to provoke "the moral outrage of the community" and the jury.

An underlying theme throughout the various arguments has been Georgia's singular role in the nation's long debate over capital punishment. In a 5-to-4 decision, the Supreme Court halted executions in 1972 because it found that judges and juries were imposing death sentences in an "arbitrary," "capricious," and "discriminatory" fashion. That landmark decision, Furman v. Georgia, came in a Georgia case. Four years later, in a momentous decision that restored the constitutional underpinnings of death penalty, the Court ruled in Gregg v. Georgia that capital punishment is constitutional if imposed according to strict procedural safeguards.

To opponents of the death penalty, the fact that blacks and other minorities continue to bear the brunt of capital punishment is evidence that little has changed since the Furman and Gregg decisions.

Bryan Stevenson, an attorney for the Southern Prisoners Defense Committee, noted that the Supreme Court said in its Gregg decision that it would not bar the death penalty without strong proof that its use was discriminatory.

"Now we're back, and we're saying, here's the proof that racial discrimination is as pervasive and invidious now as it was, and has always been," Mr. Stevenson said.

Who Decides Who Will Die? Even Within States, It Varies

BY TAMAR LEWIN | FEB. 23, 1995

AMONG THE 37 STATES with the death penalty, Texas has been the undisputed leader in executions, putting 92 people to death since the United States Supreme Court allowed capital punishment to resume in 1976.

But within Texas, the odds of a convicted killer's being put to death depend largely on where the crime took place: of those executed so far, 37 are from the Houston area, where District Attorney Johnny B. Holmes Jr. is an aggressive and vocal proponent of the death penalty. In Dallas, with a population two-thirds the size of Houston's and a District Attorney's office more cautious in its approach, only five people have been executed.

The disparity between the state's two largest cities illustrates one of the enduring truths of the nation's return to the death penalty: despite two decades of court decisions attempting to define when capital punishment is constitutional, vast differences persist in how the death penalty operates from state to state — and even county to county.

And as New York prepares to restore the death penalty, just how it will work remains an open question — both because some details of the legislation are not final and because, in practice, the use of the death penalty depends as much on prosecutors and juries as on the letter of the law.

Prosecutors' enormous discretionary power is nowhere more apparent than in two sensational murder cases now under way: in South Carolina, Susan Smith, charged with drowning her two sons, faces the death penalty, while O. J. Simpson, on trial in Los Angeles in the stabbing deaths of his former wife and a friend of hers, does not.

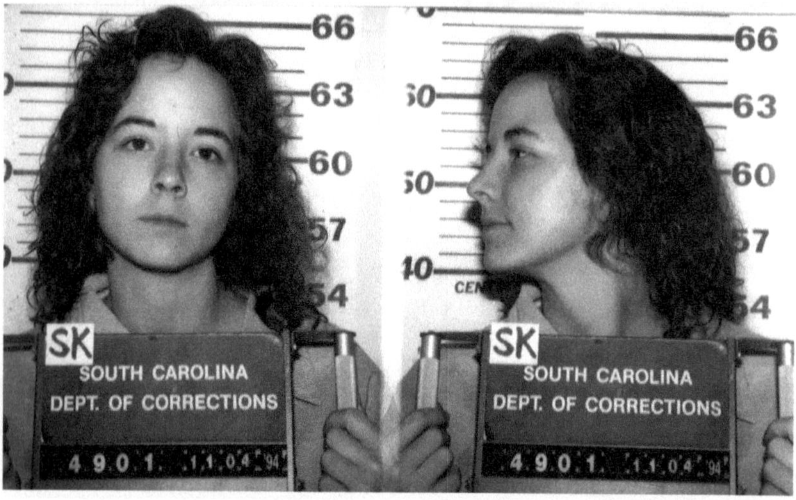

BROOKS KRAFT/SYGMA/GETTY IMAGES

Legal identity photograph of Susan Smith in 1994. She was charged with murdering her two sons, 3-year-old Michael Daniel Smith and 14-month-old Alexander Tyler Smith.

In every state with the death penalty — and experts say New York will be no exception — prosecutors seek capital punishment in only a tiny fraction of the cases in which it is allowed.

While there are some predictable patterns in how the death penalty is used, such a low proportion of the nation's murderers are executed that there are no clear-cut predictors of who will be put to death.

"There are 22,000 homicides a year, 18,000 arrests and maybe 300 death sentences, leading to maybe 50 or 60 executions," said Victor Streib, a law professor at Cleveland State University, who is assisting in Ms. Smith's defense. "How do you figure out why lightning strikes one defendant and not another? It's been studied for 20 years, and all I can say is, it's not a rational process."

Still, he and others say, there are factors that make it more likely that a particular murderer will get the death penalty.

"A key factor is what kind of attorney you can afford, so the death penalty is most commonly imposed on poor people," Mr. Streib said.

"That often correlates with people who are poorly educated, or people of color, but the issue is really less about race or class than whether they have the resources to pay lawyer fees."

And many studies have found that a killing in which the victim is white is more likely to be punished by death than one in which the victim is black.

Another important predictor is whether the crime took place in a state, and county, where the culture — and the district attorney — support capital punishment.

"In Connecticut, the death penalty is basically symbolic," said Eric Freedman, who teaches constitutional law and legal history at Hofstra University. "No one has been executed, and no one is near execution. But in the Deep South, the death penalty is a commonly used part of the criminal justice system."

Indeed, nine Southern states — Arkansas, Alabama, Florida, Georgia, Louisiana, Missouri, North Carolina, Texas and Virginia — account for 226 of the 266 people executed since the Supreme Court allowed the resumption of capital punishment in 1976. And more than a dozen states with a death penalty on the books have not executed a single criminal in that time.

LOCAL ISSUE WITHIN STATES, 'DEATH BELTS' ARISE

There are many cultural factors that come into play in determining how widely the death penalty will be used. For example, some experts suggest that in New Mexico, no one has been executed partly because the Catholic Church has spoken out against capital punishment, and many Hispanic jurors will not vote for the death penalty.

Just across the border, Texas has become the nation's leading user of the death penalty.

Stephen Bright, an Atlanta lawyer and Yale University law professor, said the attitude there reflects "a Western macho thing, the justice of the Marlboro man."

But even there, the use of the death penalty is sporadic. Of 254 counties in Texas, only 42 have put inmates on death row — and half of those counties have only a single criminal there.

But Harris County, which includes Houston, is more than well represented, accounting for 113 of the 397 inmates on the state's death row. Although Mr. Holmes, the District Attorney, would not be interviewed for this article, he has previously pronounced himself a proud supporter of the death penalty.

In Dallas, the district attorney also supports the death penalty. But Norman Kinne, the Dallas County First Assistant District Attorney responsible for deciding when to seek the death penalty, said his office seeks the death penalty only in cases where "we're 99 percent certain that's what we're going to get."

Harris County, he said, seeks death in all cases that meet the legal requirements.

"Lots of states have death belts," said James Liebman, a Columbia University law professor who is an expert on the death penalty. "In southern Georgia, there are lots of death sentences; in northern Georgia, there aren't. In Tennessee, there are tons of death sentences in Memphis and East Knoxville, but not in Nashville."

While it is difficult to predict how New York's law would be applied, experts on capital punishment are already puzzling over where in the state the death penalty is likely to be used most, and least.

In New York City, the Manhattan District Attorney, Robert M. Morgenthau, has made no secret of his opposition to capital punishment. In an article on the op-ed page of The New York Times earlier this month, he wrote that it "actually hinders the fight against crime."

But many lawyers say that the death penalty is likely to be sought relatively frequently in suburban counties, like Westchester and Nassau, where voters, and prosecutors, tend to be more conservative. They predict that upstate cities, too, will make steady use of the capital punishment law.

In Syracuse, District Attorney William Fitzpatrick, a Republican who favors the death penalty, said that he would probably seek the death penalty in about a third of the murder cases his office handles.

"I don't want to be the leading death D.A. or anything," he said. "I'd say that of the 25 murders we get each year, about two-thirds would meet the criteria for capital punishment, and off the cuff, I'd estimate that we'd seek the death penalty in half of those."

Local politics, too, often play a role, experts say. "It may depend less on the crime than on whether the prosecutor sees the case as a viable vehicle to ride into a higher elective office," said Mr. Streib of Cleveland State University.

"We had a notorious cult killing case, east of Cleveland, that helped sweep an obscure prosecutor right into Congress," he said, referring to Steven C. LaTourette, a Republican.

JURIES LOOK TO THE VICTIMS

As a practical matter, prosecutors say, the decision to bring capital charges depends in part on their sense of what juries will accept.

In the District Attorney's office in Los Angeles, Fred Sunstedt heads the Special Circumstances Committee, which decides whether to seek the death penalty. His panel reviews about 180 cases a year, and goes forward with about two dozen.

"If you have a victim who is a totally innocent child or a totally helpless older person," he said, "the jury is more likely to vote for the death penalty. But the major source of cases that come before the committee are hard-core gang shootings, drive-by shootings or drug transactions, and jurors tend to look at victims in those crimes a little differently."

And when it comes time to decide on a sentence, Mr. Sunstedt said, many jurors are not as willing to choose the death penalty as they say they will be during jury selection.

Criminal justice experts agree that the identity of the victim plays an important role in determining who will get the death penalty. When the victim is a woman or a child, capital charges are far more likely. And those who kill strangers are more apt to get the death penalty than those who kill family members, lovers or friends.

"People identify more with the victim when it's a total stranger, because that random killing is what people have the most horror of," said David Baldus, a criminal law professor at the University of Iowa who is an expert on the use of the death penalty.

Women are far less likely to get the death penalty than men, perhaps because the victims of women who kill are almost always lovers or family members. Since 1976, only one woman — a North Carolina nurse convicted of poisoning several family members — has been executed.

While mass murderers and those who torture their victims are more likely than other killers to be sentenced to death, experts say they make up only a small percentage of those on death row.

"If New York gets the death penalty, I guarantee that of the 20 people who commit the most spectacular crimes, maybe five will get death sentences, four will be reversed, and the one poor schnook who gets executed will hardly be the worst of the lot," said Mr. Freedman of Hofstra.

While opponents of the death penalty argue that it is inherently arbitrary, supporters stress the many safeguards the Supreme Court has established since 1972 to insure that it will not be capricious.

"You now have what I call 'super due process' built into the system that makes it much harder to get a death penalty," said Paul D. Kamenar, executive legal director of the Washington Legal Foundation, a conservative law and policy group. "All the laws have safeguards built in, and in some cases, I think, go overboard in making it tough for prosecutors to get capital punishment. People like Charles Manson, in cases that almost everyone would agree were particularly heinous, may not be eligible for death because they don't fit the strict categories in the state law."

Since 1972, when it ruled in Furman v. Georgia that the death penalty worked in such an arbitrary and random manner as to make it unconstitutional, the United States Supreme Court has issued opinion after opinion clarifying what is constitutionally acceptable. It has established guidelines requiring, for example, that juries must be allowed to consider evidence of mental retardation, that defendants under 16 cannot be executed, that the death penalty cannot be mandatory, and that juries must be told if there is an option of life imprisonment without parole.

The high court also requires consideration of aggravating and mitigating factors, such as the defendant's criminal record, motivation, mental or emotional disturbance, and the means of the killing.

But here, too, state laws vary. Some states do not define which factors to consider. And even states that list specific factors, as is likely in New York, emphasize different issues: in Idaho, killing without feeling is an aggravating factor, but in Arizona, it is an aggravating factor to kill with a feeling of pleasure.

VARYING CRIMES AND PUNISHMENTS

On almost every level, the death penalty differs from state to state. Even the method of execution varies, with most states favoring lethal injection, but some prescribing electrocution, hanging, the gas chamber or the firing squad.

In some states, capital punishment can be imposed for a few crimes. In New Hampshire, for example, the only crimes punishable by death are contract murder, murder of a law enforcement officer or kidnapping victim, or killing after being sentenced to life imprisonment without parole. But in many states, the death penalty can be imposed for any first-degree murder — or, in Georgia, any murder.

Experts on capital punishment say the majority of those on death row have been convicted of felony murder; that is, a killing that occurs in the course of another serious crime like robbery or kidnapping. The New York law is likely to include as capital crimes some felony murders, but not enough to make it one of the broadest in the nation.

While some states, including Texas and Georgia, give the jury the final word on whether the defendant should be sentenced to death, others, including Florida, Arizona and Alabama, leave the final decision to the judge. A few states guarantee two lawyers to defend every death penalty case, or require that lawyers handling such cases have special qualifications or training.

New Jersey — a state whose legislation New York is likely to emulate — has created an office to train, assign and oversee lawyers who handle capital cases for indigent clients.

But Texas requires no special training or qualifications, and provides no counsel beyond the first appeal. And in Louisiana, lawyers may be paid nothing at all — and may even be appointed to a case they have no interest in handling.

"They keep two lists of lawyers to appoint, a voluntary list and an involuntary one," said Mr. Bright of the Yale law school. "In some parts of Georgia, lawyers have to handle court appointments for the first five years after they're admitted to the bar, so you can get someone starting a tax practice, with no criminal experience at all, appointed to a capital case."

While Federally financed resource centers in several states struggle to provide legal representation to indigent defendants facing execution, they cannot handle all the cases. So much of the burden of handling such cases has been carried by volunteer lawyers from outside the state. But the pool of volunteers is shrinking even as the number of death penalty cases grows.

"When I started in Georgia 15 years ago, we got a lot of help from Chicago, but as capital punishment became an issue in Illinois, fewer came South," Mr. Bright said. "As Virginia's death penalty cases grew, more D.C. lawyers did their work there. When New York gets the death penalty, there's no question that a great deal of our help will disappear."

Studies Find Death Penalty Tied to Race of the Victims

BY ERIK ECKHOLM | FEB. 24, 1995

ABOUT HALF OF all the people who are murdered each year in the United States are black. Yet since 1977, when a firing squad in Utah initiated the modern era of capital punishment, the overwhelming majority of people who have been executed — 85 percent — had killed a white person.

Only 11 percent had killed a black person.

Such a huge disparity seems to suggest that racial factors may be influencing how the death penalty is dispensed — but in different ways than some people had suspected.

While death penalty opponents had long feared that the race of the killer would play a pronounced role in determining who would be executed and that blacks would be put to death far more frequently than whites, several studies suggest that the most significant distinction is the race of the victim.

Other things being equal, the studies show, killers of white people are more likely to receive death sentences than killers of blacks. This disparity, civil rights advocates say, shows that the judicial system places more value on the lives of whites than of blacks.

Whether similar racial disparities are likely to occur in New York and what, if anything, should be done to prevent it have been topics of dispute in Albany as legislators prepare to revive the death penalty.

But the experience of other states suggests to many experts that such patterns will be hard to eliminate. "Some people are being sentenced to death based on race, and I find that morally and legally objectionable," said Dr. David C. Baldus, professor of law at the University of Iowa and director of what is widely considered the most authoritative study of racial factors in capital punishment.

The question of race is among the mostly politically charged and highly studied issues in capital punishment. And it goes to the heart of a question that troubles many opponents: whether the imposition of the death penalty is inherently unfair.

Shortly before he retired from the United States Supreme Court last year, Justice Harry A. Blackmun cited intractable racial disparities as one of the reasons why he had turned against capital punishment altogether.

But bias, if it exists, is no reason to slow down executions, said Ernest van den Haag, former professor of jurisprudence at Fordham University in New York. "The fact that a murderer who gets the death penalty could point to a murderer who didn't," he said, "does not make him any less guilty."

Although the strength of some of the research findings is disputed, numerous studies around the country have reached these basic conclusions:

• Disparities in death sentencing are most often related to the race of the victim. When the victim is white, the death penalty is imposed more often whether the killer is black or white. In one study, the presence of a white victim did as much to increase the chances of a death sentence as the fact that the murder was committed during an armed robbery.

• Bias does not necessarily occur at the most visible point of the judicial process — when juries decide whether to recommend death. Often, disparities arise from earlier decisions by prosecutors, like whether to allow the defendant to plead guilty to a lesser charge or whether to ask for the death penalty at all.

• The disparities are concentrated among certain kinds of murder cases that account for perhaps one-fifth to one-fourth of the total. In a majority of murders — crimes of passion, killings in barroom brawls — death is rarely imposed. In a small number of especially grisly crimes like multiple murders, death sentences are frequent regardless of race. But for murders that fall into a middle ground — the killing of a shopkeeper in a robbery, say, or a murder by a person with a serious felony record — prosecutors and juries are more likely to agonize over the propriety of a death sentence, and hidden biases are more likely to creep in, the studies suggest.

In a 1990 review of 28 studies on race and the death penalty, the General Accounting Office in Washington said, "In 82 percent of the studies, race of victim was found to influence the likelihood of being charged with capital murder or receiving the death penalty." The office described the trend as "remarkably consistent" through research of varied quality and scope, and pointed to crucial gaps in some reports that found no bias.

The same review described as "equivocal" the evidence that the race of the defendant mattered: several studies found signs that blacks convicted of murder were more likely to be executed, especially in rural areas, but others found white defendants at higher risk, especially in cities, and some studies found no differences.

LAWS ONCE GAVE PENALTIES BY RACE

To many people, the likelihood of bias seems greatest in interracial killings, with blacks who kill whites more likely to receive death sentences. The sheer numbers appear to bear that out: over the last 18 years, 88 black men have been executed for killing whites, while only two white men have been executed for killing blacks.

But most of the studies indicate that when the nature of the crimes is taken into account as well as the fact that black-on-white killings are more frequent than white-on-black killings, the evidence of extra bias disappears. Again, the true bias arises from the race of the victim, regardless of the killer's race.

Discrimination in murder penalties by the race of the victim has a long history, especially in the South. In the days of slavery, laws in many states openly specified different penalties, said George H. Kendall, associate counsel of the NAACP Legal Defense and Educational Fund, with death the automatic sanction when a black killed a white.

"Those laws were swept away after the Civil War, but the customs that grew up around them remained," Mr. Kendall said.

In a classic 1944 study of American race relations, "An American Dilemma," Gunnar Myrdal found that when blacks committed crimes against each other without involving whites, the legal consequences were lower than when whites were harmed. "The sentences for even major crimes are ordinarily reduced when the victim is another Negro," he wrote.

Because of its size and detail, the most persuasive evidence of bias comes from a study of Georgia in the 1970's led by Dr. Baldus. Looking at 1,050 murder cases, researchers tried to weed out the influence of 39 factors that might affect penalties, from the past record of the defendant to whether the killing was committed in the course of another crime like robbery or rape to the motives and means of the killing.

After those factors are eliminated, Mr. Baldus said in a recent interview, a clear racial effect remained: when the murder victim was white, the chance of a death penalty was roughly doubled in certain kinds of cases, the ones falling into that middle ground.

JUST HOW RELIABLE ARE THE STUDIES?

Some statisticians question whether the Baldus study, let alone others of lesser sweep, really prove bias. Stephen P. Klein, a researcher at the Rand Corporation, said the available statistical methods were incapable of showing cause and effect.

He noted that the number of actual death sentences in question in such studies was small and that uncounted, often intangible factors, like the credibility of witnesses at trial, might well explain the apparent racial disparities.

Dr. Samuel R. Gross, a professor of law at the University of Michigan and an author of a study that found bias in eight states, said there was no reason to think that uncounted factors would wipe out the racial differences found in numerous studies around the country.

The focus on the race of victims, rather than defendants, has a paradoxical effect. Since most murders involve killers and victims of the same race, eliminating the disparity linked to the race of the victim would likely mean that the proportion, and perhaps the absolute number, of blacks on death row would rise.

If killers of black people were executed at the rate of killers of whites, many more blacks would receive death sentences. If, on the other hand, killers of whites were executed at the same rate as killers of blacks, many whites would be spared.

But a jump in death sentences for blacks would be unlikely, said Mr. Kendall of the legal defense fund, which opposes the death penalty on the ground that it is inherently unfair and unworkable.

"If everything were fair, I think we'd see a lot fewer capital cases over all," he said. Now, he said, the death penalty is used especially when a high-profile victim is murdered, usually a white person. Given the enormous public expense of capital cases, "we're not going to see a big increase in black victim cases," he said.

EFFORTS TO OFFSET RACIAL DISPARITIES

Whether racial disparities seen in other parts of country will extend to New York when it institutes the death penalty cannot be known. Dr. Baldus and others caution against assuming that studies in one place and time apply to any other. But he added that his recent analysis of death sentencing in New Jersey in the 1980's produced preliminary evidence of similar bias, though the numbers are still small.

Mr. Kendall said that if anything, the country appeared to be moving backward in race relations and that prejudice was by no means limited to the South. "I don't see anything about New York that would make the process work any differently here than anywhere else," he said.

What might be done to purge the death penalty of bias is unclear. As one countermeasure, New York legislators apparently plan, in capital cases, to permit lawyers to question potential jurors in private about their racial attitudes.

New York may also call for research on racial aspects of death-sentencing over time to detect any disparities. But it apparently will not take the step that civil rights advocates want most: to write into the law that statistical evidence of disparities should be a powerful weapon in court for individual defendants facing death.

If prosecutors had no legitimate explanation for detected disparities, Mr. Kendall said, then death sentences in the affected subgroup of defendants should be overturned.

The Baldus study itself was the centerpiece of an appeal to the United States Supreme Court in 1987 by a black man in Georgia who had been sentenced to death for murdering a white police officer. In the case, McCleskey v. Kemp, the defendant argued that his penalty should be revoked, based on the evidence of systematic discrimination in cases like his.

The Supreme Court, by a 5-to-4 vote, rejected the appeal, arguing that he also had to prove actual discrimination in the handling of his own case.

But defense lawyers say that that standard has harmed their search for racial fairness.

"It's almost impossible to prove purposeful discrimination in a single case," said Dale Jones, an assistant public defender in Trenton.

For the last several years, civil rights groups have sought to write a "racial justice" provision into Federal criminal law, which would require quantitative studies of racial patterns in death sentencing and give powerful courtroom standing to any findings. But last year, Congress, as it adopted a new crime bill, rejected the proposal. Opponents belittled the evidence of bias and said such a law could be used in court to bog down any application of the death penalty.

Dr. van den Haag, the death penalty proponent, questioned the importance of research showing bias by the race of the victim. And even if discrimination exists, he said, the solution is not to abolish the death penalty but to end disparities — by increasing executions of the favored group.

Dr. Baldus said the issue was not whether blacks or whites get their share of death sentences but whether justice is tainted by inappropriate considerations. "The real concern isn't the number of black people on death row," he said. "It's the integrity of the system."

Rethinking the Death Penalty

BY BARBARA FITZGERALD | DEC. 14, 2003

THE RAIN WAS falling softly outside as David Kaczynski talked about the day he had to tell his mother that F.B.I. agents suspected her eldest son of being the Unabomber. The cadence of his speech revealed the unremitting pain of a man who could still not figure out how an esteemed older brother had become a cold-blooded killer who mounted a crusade against progress.

Seven years later, the guilt of turning his only sibling, Theodore J. Kaczynski, over to the authorities still haunts him. But the reason he is speaking to a crowd gathered at Xavier Center, a retreat and conference center affiliated with the Sisters of Charity of St. Elizabeth, in the town of Convent Station, has more to do with strangers, killers he has never met.

Mr. Kaczynski's message is clear. However heinous the crime or

RICH PEDRONCELLI/AFP/GETTY IMAGES

David Kaczynski, left, stands next to his mother, Wanda, as he speaks to the media during his brother Ted's trial on Jan. 22, 1998. Ted pleaded guilty the next day.

troubled the mind, those on death row are the brothers, the fathers and the sons of people who — depending on prestige or skin color — often find themselves victims of disparate forms of justice.

Theodore Kaczynski escaped the death sentence with the help of smart, expensive lawyers who arranged a plea agreement to spare his life, his brother explained. "My brother had the two best lawyers in the country," the younger Mr. Kaczynski said. "No one on death row had lawyers like my brother."

As New Jersey moves closer to executing someone for the first time in more than three decades, Mr. Kaczynski's talk is especially compelling for those who believe that New Jersey's law on capital punishment needs to be re-examined. Though there are now 14 people on death row at Trenton State Prison, no one has been put to death since New Jersey reinstituted capital punishment in 1982.

In 1968, the last time New Jersey executed someone, reporters and witnesses sat within a few feet of the electric chair, now a museum relic at the State Police barracks in Ewing. Shortly before his death, the prisoner, Ralph Hudson, had prime rib dinner, a cigar and the chance to talk with a clergyman. There was a steady stream of protesters outside, but no last-minute stays.

Protesters are still at the gates. Federal appeals are running out for John Martini, who was convicted in the 1989 shooting of Irving Flax, a Fair Lawn businessman. But New Jersey legislators, responding with a newfound sensitivity because of grievous errors committed in the death penalty system and concerns over costs of the appeals process, are re-examining the law in an effort to delay any future executions for at least a year and a half.

Last week, legislators passed a measure calling for a bipartisan commission to examine the cost, fairness and effects of capital prosecutions. So far, Governor McGreevey says he does not see the need for such a study, though he has stopped short of saying whether he will veto the measure. If the study goes forward, it will mark a big change from the way the death penalty was viewed during the administration of Gov. Christie Whitman. In 1997, on the 15th anniversary of the reinstatement of the death penalty, Mrs. Whitman wanted to know why it was taking the state so long to execute those on death row.

Under New Jersey's death penalty law a jury must first determine a defendant's guilt and then in a separate trial decide whether the defendant should be executed or given a life sentence, which means at least 30 years in prison before parole eligibility.

In the second phase of the trial, the jury is asked to weigh aggravating factors, like the defendant's record, the "wanton and vile" nature of the crime, including whether the defendant intended to torture the victim before the murder and whether the defendant hired someone to commit the murder.

Mitigating factors include lack of a previous criminal record, testimony about the defendant's character and evidence that the defendant did not intend the death of the victim. The State Supreme Court has said aggravating factors must outweigh mitigating factors beyond a reasonable doubt before a death sentence can be applied.

Once a person is sentenced to die, there are many appeals procedures to determine if the death sentence was fairly applied and to ensure that it was fitting for the crime.

Governor Whitman's study commission believed the execution process had become too bogged down through appeals. The group called for the elimination of an extra layer of appeals, known as "proportionality review," which requires the court to determine whether the death sentence is appropriate when compared with other murder cases. But the commission, while sounding a popular theme at the time to get tougher with criminals, failed to persuade the Legislature to enact many of its suggestions. But the state Supreme Court did act to streamline the appeals process in 1999 in an attempt to speed up executions.

SENTIMENT IS SHIFTING

Now the tide has shifted once again. As headlines nationwide reveal errors in the death penalty process, it appears that New Jersey is also in the mood to take a closer look at its system to ensure that the sentencing is fair and accurate.

Because of advances in forensic science, Gov. Mitt Romney of Massachusetts recently appointed a council to write a law that would restore capital punishment in his state — one of 12 that have abandoned it — while requiring physical evidence of guilt that would meet "the highest evidentiary standard" before a death sentence could be imposed. And in Illinois, Gov. George Ryan imposed a moratorium on the death penalty in 2000, which is still in place while the state legislature debates recommendations on improving the process, after 13 death row inmates were found to have been wrongfully convicted.

Although no one on New Jersey's death row has been exonerated, 27 people on death rows in other states have been cleared of their crimes since 2000, according to the Death Penalty Information Center in Washington.

As recently as last week, prosecutors in Pennsylvania announced they were dropping all charges against a man who had been on death row for 21 years, Nicholas Yarris, after DNA tests were performed.

"There have been so many developments as a result of new technologies that have exposed the fact that sometimes eyewitnesses get it wrong, and sometimes jailhouse snitches lie," said Celeste Fitzgerald, a founding chairwoman of New Jerseyans for a Death Penalty Moratorium, a group formed in 1999 that claims 10,000 members and has the support of more than 200 groups, including many faith-based organizations.

"There's an awareness that we might not always get it right and that no system is infallible. When it comes to the death penalty, people are not willing to accept mistakes, not when a life is on the line."

Still, former Representative Dick Zimmer, who was chairman of the panel established by Governor Whitman, known formally as the Study Commission on the Implementation of the Death Penalty, said in a recent interview that he saw no reason for another study, and that there was no need to delay executions any longer.

Mr. Zimmer said New Jersey's system was fair — probably one of the fairest in the nation — because of the strength of the public defender's office and a state Supreme Court that has historically been reluctant to uphold death sentences.

Indeed, he said that the state Supreme Court did not uphold a death sentence until 1991 — nearly 10 years after the state had re-enacted it.

"As a freshman assemblyman, I never dreamed this legislation I voted for would be in effect for so long and yet not result in a single execution," he said.

The way he sees it, it is "just as wrong for a guilty person to avoid lawful punishment as it is for an innocent person to be convicted."

But other lawmakers have come to different conclusions.

State Senator Robert Martin, a Republican of Morris Plains, said he believed it might be time for New Jersey to consider a complete ban on capital executions — though not entirely for humanitarian reasons. Mr. Martin said that New Jersey's review process "is so cumbersome and expensive" that the state might be better off "with a punishment that was life imprisonment without parole."

Recent public opinion surveys suggest that when respondents are asked to consider the alternative of life without the chance of parole, only 36 percent of those polled in New Jersey actually support capital punishment. That is a sharp departure from what residents thought about capital punishment just decades ago.

According to the archives of the Eagleton Poll at Rutgers University, 76 percent of those questioned supported the death penalty in 1975. In 1981, 73 percent said they were in favor of the death penalty, and by 1999 that number had dropped to 63 percent.

"It's continually gone down over the years," said Patrick Murray, associate director of the Star-Ledger/Eagleton Poll. "We keep seeing a steady erosion of support for the death penalty."

Mr. Murray said that it was not that New Jerseyans were soft on crime, but that they wanted to make sure the system was fairly applied and that those who had committed heinous crimes would not be walking the streets in 20 or 30 years.

For his part, Ed Martone, executive director of the New Jersey Association on Correction, an advocacy for prisoners, said he was not sure New Jersey residents were ready to resume executions.

"If you look at the jury selection in capital cases, it's what is called the 'death eligible' jury," Mr. Martone said. "It's people who have said, 'No, I don't have any philosophical objections to the death penalty. I think I could under certain circumstances vote for a death sentence.' And yet even in those situations, a good number of people have said, " 'Well, I couldn't do it. When faced with my vote, I couldn't do it.' "

Aside from the question of the popularity of capital punishment, critics say, the problem with the death penalty in New Jersey is that too often it is not applied fairly.

QUESTIONS OF FAIRNESS

A study commissioned in 2001 by the state Supreme Court found evidence that "strongly suggests that defendants who kill white victims are more likely to advance to a death penalty trial than defendants who kill African-American victims."

Mr. Martone said the proposed study commission now before the Legislature should ask why a prosecutor in one case decides to seek a life sentence, and yet in another decides to go for a death sentence. Often, he said, "there's an appearance that in case Number One the victim is white and in case Number Two the defendant is black."

Critics also say the odds of receiving a death sentence vary widely from county to county.

"Why is it if I commit a murder in Monmouth County I get a death sentence and if I commit a murder in Essex County I get a life sentence?" Mr. Martone asked.

In 2001, after the state Supreme Court findings were released, State Attorney General John J. Farmer ordered a review of the standards used by prosecutors in seeking the death penalty, but he and Mrs. Whitman left office before the review could be completed.

Those who have lobbied legislators for the new study commission say that geography, the influence of families of the victim, the race of the victim and the ability of attorneys representing the suspect can also influence the decision on whether to seek the death penalty.

They also say the proposed study will be the first in the nation to comprehensively look at all of the issues surrounding the death penalty. After the study is completed, it is very likely that voters will be asked whether the state should spend millions of tax dollars on appeals or simply recommend life imprisonment.

For all of these reasons, said Sandra Manning, chairwoman of New Jerseyans for a Death Penalty Moratorium, efforts to pass a bill to suspend all executions "reflects the overwhelming public and political support for a thorough study of New Jersey's death penalty."

"New Jerseyans have demonstrated genuine concern about capital punishment, including the way it is applied," Ms. Manning said.

Currently there are 14 men on death row — 6 black and 8 white. Some cases have received much notoriety, such as that of Robert Marshall, a business executive from Toms River, who was convicted of hiring a gunman to shoot his wife to death on the Garden State Parkway in 1984.

Others have received attention because of the heinousness of the crime. For instance, Jesse K. Timmendaquas, a repeat sex offender, was found guilty and sentenced to die in 1997 for the rape and murder of Megan Kanka in 1994. Mr. Timmendaquas lured the 8-year-old Ms. Kanka into his house in Hamilton with the promise of showing her a new puppy.

Yet there are those who committed crimes of equal brutality who escaped the death sentence.

'THE LUCK OF THE DRAW'

"I have in my office a book with narrative descriptions of cases that could have been or were prosecuted as a capital offense," said Lawrence Lustberg, a defense lawyer in Newark. "You cannot meaningfully distinguish between those who received the death penalty and those who did not. There are horribly heinous rapes and murders all the time that escape capital prosecution. It is exceedingly arbitrary. It depends on the luck of the draw and the county that you commit the crime."

It was the arbitrary nature of such death sentences decades ago that brought a temporary halt to executions across the country.

The 1972 landmark case Furman v. Georgia — which set the stage for a new generation of death penalty laws and divided capital cases into two phases — involved a burglar who accidentally shot and killed someone after he tripped while fleeing the scene of the crime. The United States Supreme Court ruled that Georgia's death penalty law constituted "cruel and unusual punishment," which violated the Constitution because of the arbitrary manner in which it was imposed. It also said that it indicated a racial bias against the defendants. That decision forced states to reconsider their death penalty statutes to ensure they were not administered in a capricious or discriminatory manner.

Former Gov. Brendan J. Byrne, who is a also a former judge and Essex County prosecutor, remains an ardent opponent of the death penalty.

In an address given to critics of the death penalty in 2000, Mr. Byrne said that he recalled how arbitrary the death penalty could be applied.

"I remember one case where I withdrew a recommendation for the death penalty," he said, "because the attorney for the defendant was having a nervous breakdown.

While Mr. Byrne was governor, the Legislature tried to re-enact the death penalty twice. He vetoed both attempts.

"There were clear attempts on the part of the Legislature to override those vetoes and in each case my veto was sustained," he said. "So we did not have a death penalty during the eight years that I was governor."

Mr. Byrne, who is also remembered as the governor who established the state income tax, said, "People were mad at me for a lot of other things, but I think I was able to defend my position on the death penalty without it costing me any political capital."

Washington State Supreme Court Deems Death Penalty Unconstitutional

BY KIRK JOHNSON | OCT. 11, 2018

SEATTLE — Washington became the latest state to end the death penalty on Thursday, following a scathing State Supreme Court decision that declared the practice unconstitutional. The ruling commuted the sentences of the eight men currently on the state's death row to life in prison and made Washington the 20th state where courts or legislatures have abolished or overturned capital punishment.

A five-member majority on the State Supreme Court did not say that executing people who commit heinous crimes is inherently wrong, but said evidence showed that death sentences had been "imposed in an arbitrary and racially biased manner." Four other justices concurred with the conclusion in a separate, equally sweeping decision.

"We are confident that the association between race and the death penalty is not attributed to random chance," the majority's decision said. The finding grew out of an appeal brought by Allen Eugene Gregory, a black man who was convicted of the rape, robbery and murder of a waitress named Geneine Harshfield in 1996. Mr. Gregory, 46, was sentenced to death in 2001.

Use of the death penalty has been in decline across the nation for nearly two decades, and Washington has not executed anyone since 2010. In 2014, Gov. Jay Inslee, a Democrat, ordered a moratorium on all executions.

Capital punishment remains legal in 30 states, and is also allowed by the federal government and the United States military. But the number of death sentences actually imposed has steadily fallen since a peak in 1999, when there were 98 executions across the nation, according to the Death Penalty Information Center. In 2017, there were 23. Only 10 states, including Texas, Ohio and Florida, have carried out any executions since 2014.

In its decision, the Washington Supreme Court said that death as a penalty for crime is not in itself unconstitutional, but that the law as it has been written by the Legislature and applied by judges and juries was too deeply flawed to continue.

"We leave open the possibility that the Legislature may enact a 'carefully drafted statute,' " the majority wrote. "But it cannot create a system that offends constitutional rights."

Mr. Inslee said in a news conference that he would veto any bill that attempted to reinstate the death penalty or to fix the flaws outlined by the justices. And the state attorney general, Bob Ferguson, a Democrat, said the court's decision would reinvigorate his efforts to urge lawmakers to permanently repeal the death penalty from statute books.

"We should act quickly to remove the death penalty from state law once and for all," he said in a statement. "Next session, I will again propose legislation repealing the death penalty, replacing it with life in prison without the possibility of parole."

Since 2009, five states — New Mexico, Illinois, Connecticut and Maryland and Nebraska — have repealed the death penalty, according to the National Conference of State Legislatures, though Nebraska's was reinstated by a statewide vote in 2016.

In its 42-page ruling, Washington's Supreme Court referred repeatedly to a study completed by researchers at the University of Washington, who examined the role of race in convictions between 1981 to 2014. "In aggravated murder cases, jurors are more than four times more likely to impose a death sentence if the defendant is black," the study concluded.

Decisions by prosecutors to seek the death penalty varied widely. In one county, prosecutors sought the death penalty in 67 percent of aggravated murder cases, while prosecutors in another county didn't pursue that punishment even once, the study found. Of the eight men who have been on Washington State's death row, five are white and three are black.

Four of the Washington State justices concurred with the conclusion in a separate opinion.

"Where a system exists permeated with arbitrary decision-making, random imposition of the death penalty, unreliability, geographic rarity and excessive delays, such a system cannot constitutionally stand," the four justices wrote.

CHAPTER 3

From Furman to Gregg, a Brief Moratorium on Executions

The most successful effort to abolish capital punishment came in 1972. In Furman v. Georgia, the Supreme Court found the application of the death penalty to be arbitrary and capricious, thus constituting "cruel and unusual punishment" in violation of the Eighth Amendment. The moratorium on executions lasted until 1976, when in Gregg v. Georgia, the Court found several states' new sentencing procedures for the death penalty to be constitutional, allowing executions to resume.

An End to the Death Penalty

OPINION | BY ARTHUR J. GOLDBERG AND ALAN M. DERSHOWITZ | JUNE 6, 1971

WE ARE IN THE MIDST of a great national debate over capital punishment. The debate is being carried on in the legislative, executive and judicial chambers of our state and national governments. Since June 2, 1967, there have been no official executions in our land.

Although the Supreme Court of the United States recently answered some questions about the role of the jury in capital cases, the Court has never decided the underlying and fundamental question: whether the death penalty is constitutionally permissible under the "cruel and unusual punishment" clause of the Eighth Amendment.

Meanwhile, the decision finally to abolish capital punishment has yet to be made in most jurisdictions and death sentences continue to be imposed. The lives of about 650 prisoners waiting in death row are immediately at stake. At stake also is our faith in and commitment to national self-improvement, as we decide whether to take what Camus called the "great civilizing step" of abolishing the death penalty.

Despite the absence of any proof that the death penalty actually deters crime, the issue remains a highly emotional one. Further, as the reaction to the latest Supreme Court decision on the subject indicates, many legislative, and executive policy makers, seem to feel restrained from making their own constitutional interpretation on the issue and look to the Supreme Court alone for its resolution.

In describing the relative roles of the Court and the other departments of Government, one must begin with a proposition fundamental to our system of government: "The Constitution, as interpreted by the Court, is the supreme law of the land." Once the Supreme Court has decided that certain basic rights are constitutionally protected, these protections may not be diminished by any other department, Federal or state. But there is nothing in our system of government which precludes the other branches from extending the spirit of constitutional protections beyond what the Court has mandated. As Judge Learned Hand observed, the Constitution is "admonitory or hortatory." What it "does not command, it may still inspire."

Under Section Five of the Fourteenth Amendment, Congress may enforce the constitutional protections secured by that amendment against violations by the states. In Katzenbach v. Morgan, the New York English literacy requirement case, the Supreme Court recently held that Congress may interpret the equal-protection clause of the Fourteenth Amendment more expansively than would the Supreme Court itself and may then enforce that interpretation on the states. The Court in Morgan required only that it be able to "perceive a basis" for Congress's constitutional interpretation. The same reasoning, it seems to us, should apply to a Congressional interpretation of the Fourteenth Amendment (absorbing the cruel and unusual punishment clause of the Eighth Amendment) declaring the death penalty unconstitutional. Thus, at one blow, Congress, under this theory, might abolish capital punishment throughout the United States. In any event, under this and a number of other legal theories, there would seem to be little doubt of the authority of Congress to declare a two-year moratorium on death penalties, as proposed by Senator Hart and Representative Celler.

Of course, absent Congressional action, state legislatures may without inhibition, as some have done, eliminate the death penalty because of their conviction that the death penalty today in their opinion is cruel and unusual punishment and, therefore, unconstitutional. And there is nothing in constitutional theory that would or should restrain them from so doing regardless of what the Supreme Court may or may not do in this regard.

In practical terms, however, it may well be that the immediate responsibility will lie with state governors, who have the complete authority to dispense executive clemency and who are free to grant clemency on their conviction that the death penalty today is unconstitutional.

If the 648 men and women in death row — or any substantial portion of them — are sent to their deaths, capital punishment will have been revived as the active penal policy of the United States. The specter of mass execution — following a moratorium of four years — threatens to further brutalize a nation already saturated with war, riots and crime. This generation of Americans has experienced enough killing. Official execution must be ended. And it can be ended, even if the Supreme Court does not intervene in these cases. Fidelity to constitutional principle certainly permits — indeed, in our view, it requires — the end to all death sentences.

ARTHUR J. GOLDBERG is a former Justice of the Supreme Court. **ALAN M. DERSHOWITZ** is professor of law at Harvard Law School and was law clerk to Mr. Goldberg during the 1963 term of the Supreme Court.

California Ruling on Capital Punishment

LETTER | THE NEW YORK TIMES | FEB. 27, 1972

In a series of letters to the editor published between February and April 1972, two Times readers would argue over the constitutionality of the death penalty. What immediately follows is the first of these three letters, in which Richard H. Wels opposes the California Supreme Court's decision in California v. Anderson. Subsequently comes a challenge from a professor of constitutional law by the name of Leo Pfeffer and Mr. Wels's response to Mr. Pfeffer.

To the Editor:

THE DECISION OF the California Supreme Court striking down the death penalty as cruel and unusual punishment is an extreme example of judicial legislation.

In 1888 New York enacted a law providing that the death penalty must in all cases be inflicted by electrocution. That statute was challenged on various bases, including that it provided for cruel and unusual punishment. The Supreme Court in Kemmler, 136 U.S. 436, 446, sustained the statute and specifically said:

"Punishments are cruel when they involve torture or a lingering death; but the punishment of death is not cruel, within the meaning of that word as used in the Constitution. It implies there something inhuman and barbarous, something more than the mere extinguishment of life." That the Constitution does not prohibit the death penalty is evident from the language of the Fourteenth Amendment that no state shall deprive any person of life, liberty or property without due process of law.

In 1947 the Supreme Court again had occasion to consider the death penalty in the case of Willie Francis, who had been convicted of murder in Louisiana and had been electrocuted as directed by the courts.

He survived his electrocution and then brought proceedings to restrain Louisiana from another and more successful electrocution.

The Supreme Court denied him relief, saying: "The cruelty against which the Constitution protects a convicted man is cruelty inherent in the method of punishment, not the necessary suffering involved in any method employed to extinguish life humanely."

There are many valid arguments for the abolition of the death penalty that would warrant its repeal by legislation. But this does not justify judges, impatient with legislative delays, taking the law into their own hands and legislating themselves.

RICHARD H. WELS
New York, Feb. 21, 1972

Why the Death Penalty Must Be Abolished

LETTER | THE NEW YORK TIMES | MARCH 12, 1972

To the Editor:

IN HIS LETTER of Feb. 27, Richard H. Wels asserts that since the Constitution forbids deprivation of life, liberty or property without due process of law, it implicitly allows capital punishment notwithstanding the Eighth Amendment's prohibition of cruel and unusual punishments.

This reasoning, however, proves too much. The Constitution also provides that no person shall "be subject for the same offense to be twice put in jeopardy of life or limb," thus implying that dismemberment (e.g., cutting off an ear, which was actually practiced when the Constitution was written) is permissible so long as it is imposed only once for the same offense. Yet would anyone expect the Supreme Court to uphold such punishment today?

When the Eighth Amendment was added to our Constitution the death penalty was deemed an acceptable form of punishment for many different crimes, including, for example, passing forged Government securities. But that fact would hardly be conclusive today in interpreting and applying the Eighth Amendment.

The crux of the matter was stated by Chief Justice Warren in the 1959 case of Trop v. Dulles. "The amendment," he said, "must draw its meaning from the evolving standards of decency that mark the progress of maturing society."

The California Supreme Court, which Mr. Wels criticized, adjudged rightly that whatever may have been the case when the Constitution was written, under contemporary standards of decency, capital punishment is no longer acceptable.

LEO PFEFFER
Professor of Constitutional Law, Long Island University
Brooklyn, Feb. 28, 1972

Legality of Death Penalty

LETTER | THE NEW YORK TIMES | APRIL 2, 1972

To the Editor:

JUDGING FROM HIS March 12 letter, "Why the Death Penalty Must Be Abolished," Prof. Leo Pfeffer does not believe, as did the late Mr. Justice Black, that the Constitution must be understood to mean what it says. The constitutional prohibition against the deprivation of life, liberty and property without due process of law is as clear as the provision that Congress shall make no law abridging the freedom of the press.

The opinion of Chief Justice Warren in Trop v. Dulles, is not a likely authority to cite in support of the proposition that capital punishment offends the prohibition of the Eighth Amendment of cruel and unusual punishments. It was in that opinion that the Chief Justice said after noting that there were "forceful" arguments against capital punishment: "...the death penalty has been employed throughout our history, and, in a day when it is still widely accepted, it cannot be said to violate the constitutional concept of cruelty..."

There are indeed forceful arguments that can be made for the abolition of capital punishment — but they should be made to the legislatures and not to the courts. Not only do the courts not have the constitutional competence to act upon such arguments, they lack the ability to provide an adequate substitute.

The California Supreme Court, holding the death penalty to be unconstitutional, has substituted life imprisonment instead. But in California life imprisonment means not life imprisonment but a term of years. Is it acceptable that the community be faced in a few years with dealing with a Sirhan Sirhan and a Charles Manson at large again?

RICHARD H. WELS
New York, March 27, 1972

Court Spares 600

BY FRED P. GRAHAM | JUNE 30, 1972

WASHINGTON, JUNE 29 — The Supreme Court ruled today that capital punishment, as now administered in the United States, is unconstitutional "cruel and unusual" punishment.

The historic decision, came on a vote of 5 to 4.

Although the five Justices in the majority issued separate opinions and did not agree on a single reason for their action, the effect of the decision appeared to be to rule out executions under any capital punishment laws now in effect in this country.

The decision will also save from execution 600 condemned men and women now on death rows in the United States, although it did not

BETTMANN/GETTY IMAGES

In Furman v. Georgia (1972), the Supreme Court ruled 5-4 that capital punishment, as employed at the time, was unconstitutional. All of the justices except William O. Douglas (front row, second from left) were still on the court four years later when new procedures were ruled constitutional, allowing executions to resume.

overturn their convictions. Most will be held in prison for the rest of their lives, but under some states' procedures some of the prisoners may eventually gain their freedom.

EIGHTH AMENDMENT CITED

The decision pitted the five holdovers of the more liberal Warren Court against the four appointees of President Nixon, who dissented. The ruling came as the Supreme Court handed down its final decisions of the year and recessed until Oct. 2.

Three Justices in the majority, William O. Douglas, William J. Brennan Jr. and Thurgood Marshall, concluded that executions in modern-day America necessarily violate the Eighth Amendment's prohibition against "cruel and unusual punishments."

The other two in the majority, the two "swing men" of the Court, Justices Potter Stewart and Byron R. White, reasoned that the present legal system operates in a cruel and unusual way, because it gives judges and juries the discretion to decree life or death and they impose it erratically.

As Justice Stewart put it, the death penalty is "so wantonly and so freakishly imposed" that those who are sentenced to death receive excessively harsh treatment.

VIEW OF CHIEF JUSTICE

"These death sentences are cruel and unusual in the same way that being struck by lightning is cruel and unusual," he said.

As the dissenters pointed out, this alignment means that no death sentence can pass muster before the present Supreme Court unless it satisfies the objections voiced by Justices Stewart and White.

Chief Justice Warren E. Burger suggested that legislatures could attempt to do this in two ways. One is to state in statute books in detail the conditions under which a judge or jury can impose the death penalty — such as rape accompanied by a vicious assault, or a convict's murder of a prison guard.

The second would be to revert to the practice of more than a century ago, and impose mandatory death sentences for those convicted of certain crimes.

In any event, Chief Justice Burger said, Congress and the state legislatures will be required to "make a thorough reevaluation of the entire subject of capital punishment," including a serious inquiry into whether it serves as a deterrent.

All four dissenters also filed separate opinions, in a judicial outpouring that required 243 pages to express the view of all nine Justices.

The gist of the dissenters' position was that the Eighth Amendment has been in effect for 191 years and has not, until today, been held to rule out executions. They charged that the majority had usurped the prerogative of the legislatures in the decision today.

Justice Lewis F. Powell Jr. said the action would have a "shattering effect" upon the rule that prior decisions should be followed, as well as on the principles of "Federalism, judicial restraint, and — most importantly — separation of powers."

DECISION IN CALIFORNIA

Justice Harry A. Blackmun implied strongly that the majority had been "propelled toward its result" to strike down capital punishment by the recent decision of the Supreme Court of California, which outlawed executions under the state constitution's prohibition against "cruel or unusual" punishments.

Justice Blackmun added an unusually personal insight by saying that while he had an "abhorrence" of capital punishment he felt only the legislatures could abolish it.

Justice William H. Rehnquist's dissent said the decision had underscored a fundamental question about the Supreme Court's role in reviewing the nation's laws. While overreaching legislatures may encroach upon individual rights, he said, an overreaching Supreme Court can "sacrifice the equally important right of the people to govern themselves."

The decision today culminated a campaign initiated by the N.A.A.C.P. Legal Defense and Educational Fund, Inc., five years ago, when the liberal coloration of the Warren Court made success appear much more likely than it had been presumed to be before the present Court.

Although the Supreme Court had never directly ruled that the death penalty was not cruel and unusual punishment, this was because it had been assumed throughout most of the country's history that it was not. The Court had said so, in passing, without actually making a ruling to that effect.

In his 50-page concurring opinion today, Justice William J. Brennan Jr. traced the evolution of the "cruel and unusual" punishment concept, and pointed out that the Supreme Court has traditionally considered it a growing concept, which develops with the changing mores of the times.

Therefore, even though the framers of the Bill of Rights did not intend to outlaw executions when they adopted the Eighth Amendment, Justice Brennan asserted that present conditions bring the death penalty within the prohibition.

His reasoning was that the penalty was unusually severe and degrading, it appeared to be arbitrarily imposed. It was widely condemned by contemporary society, and it might be no better a deterrent than prison.

Justice Thurgood Marshall expressed similar arguments, adding that the penalty was "morally unacceptable," if for no other reason than that it most frequently fell upon blacks, "the poor, the ignorant, and the underprivileged members of society."

Justice Douglas asserted that it is "implicit" in the ban on cruel and unusual punishment that executions cannot be imposed indiscriminately. Because it is the poor and minority groups that most often are executed, he concluded, capital punishment violates the 14th Amendment's guarantee of equal protection of the laws, as well as the Eighth Amendment.

Prior to today's decision, 11 state legislatures had abolished capital punishment completely, or with such narrow exceptions as the murder of a prison guard by a life convict. Thirty-nine states, the District of Columbia and the Federal Government had laws that authorized executions for various crimes.

The defendants before the Court today were William Henry Furman, sentenced to death for a robbery-murder in Georgia, and Lucius Jackson Jr. of Georgia and Elmer Branch of Texas, both condemned to death for rape.

Anthony G. Amsterdam, a professor of law at Stanford University, and Jack Greenberg of New York argued the cases for the legal defense fund. Melvyn C. Bruder of Dallas also argued against the death penalty.

The prosecutors who argued the other side were Mrs. Dorothy T. Beasley, Assistant Attorney General of Georgia, and Prof. Charles Alan Wright of the University of Texas.

In another decision the Court held, 8 to 1, that a parolee who has been returned to prison for violation of parole must be given a prompt hearing, with notice of the reasons for the revocation and an opportunity to cross-examine witnesses against him.

Justice Douglas dissented, saying that a parolee should not be returned to prison until after his hearing. He also gave his answer to a point that the Court left open, saying he believes a parolee should have counsel furnished by the state, if necessary, at such a hearing.

Death Again in California

OPINION | BY TOM WICKER | NOV. 12, 1972

WASHINGTON — Among other singular works of the people in last week's election was the strong vote in California, the most populous state, for Proposition Seventeen, the restoration of the death penalty. This raises numerous questions, in addition to the old, familiar argument as to whether capital punishment itself is ineffective and immoral.

The death penalty was held unconstitutional in California last February, by the California Supreme Court's interpretation of the California Constitution. This court held that imposition of the death penalty was both cruel and unusual and therefore unconstitutional. Later this year, the Federal Supreme Court, interpreting the Federal Constitution, held in Furman v. Georgia that a capital sentence was unconstitutional in cases where the jury or the court had discretion to impose a lesser penalty — that the death penalty was not in itself necessarily cruel or unusual but that to impose it arbitrarily and capriciously was impermissible.

Therefore, although Californians voted to overrule their own Supreme Court and restore the death penalty, they had no power to overrule the Federal Supreme Court; so they could re-establish capital punishment in California only to the extent permitted under the Furman v. Georgia ruling. That is, the death penalty can be imposed only when the law makes it mandatory.

Before the California court ruling last February, the state had made death mandatory for only four crimes: train wrecking, perjury in a capital case, treason against the state and the murder of a prison guard or any non-inmate by a life-term prisoner. So the referendum vote could restore the death penalty only for these crimes of which the last became one of the rallying points for proponents of Proposition Seventeen. How could a life-term prisoner be deterred from killing a guard, they asked, if his only punishment would be another life term of the first?

The question now is whether the California Legislature will make the death sentence mandatory — the only way in which it can be constitutional — for other crimes, say, rape or first-degree murder or selling heroin. If so, there are sure to be many cases in which death will be an inappropriate and outrageous — yet mandatory — penalty. Knowing this, will juries acquit, in some cases, rather than convict when the death penalty is certain? And some lawyers argue that since a capital case is usually subject to perhaps five separate appeals the renewed use of the death penalty — particularly when it is mandatory — will impose a huge new burden on courts and prosecutors.

To the extent, moreover, that the Legislature does make the death penalty mandatory for certain crimes in California, Proposition Seventeen would prevent judicial review, since it states that capital punishment "shall not be deemed" to violate any part of the California Constitution. This raises in sharpest form the question of the separation of powers.

Proponents of Proposition Seventeen had argued that in ruling the death penalty unconstitutional the California Supreme Court had usurped an essentially legislative function — since that was the first instance in which capital punishment had been barred by judicial review rather than by legislation. Now, however, Proposition Seventeen has specifically prevented the courts from reviewing what the California Legislature may do about capital punishment.

That is not far from what the Nixon Administration is asking Congress to do on the question of busing — to pass a law saying what the courts may or may not do, what remedies they may or may not impose for unconstitutional racial discrimination. And on another point having to do with highway construction, even Chief Justice Burger has invited Congress to pass legislation barring judicial review.

In the case of the death penalty in California, the net effect of Proposition Seventeen is that the people overruled the court as to the meaning of the state's Bill of Rights, then further limited the court's power to review the constitutionality of future legislative action. Those who support the death penalty, even those who argue that "elitists" on the courts and elsewhere have been thwarting the will of the people, ought to think long and hard about the implications of that vote.

It is not just that California's action may lead other state legislatures, citing public opinion in the most populous state as their justification, into a flurry of mandatory death sentence laws. If Congress and the legislatures, always sensitive barometers of public opinion, begin limiting the power of the courts to review the validity of legislative acts, they could destroy or badly impair the courts' important function of protecting unpopular principles, unpowerful people and unconforming activities from rampant majoritarianism.

TOM WICKER is an Op-Ed columnist for The New York Times.

Court to Review Death Penalty Issue

BY LESLEY OELSNER | JAN. 23, 1976

Here, The Times first reports on the Gregg v. Georgia case, in which the Supreme Court would find that several states' revised statutes outlining new guidelines for imposing the death penalty were, indeed, constitutional. The article reporting on the case's decision, which included a historical overview of the death penalty in the United States, follows.

WASHINGTON, JAN. 22 — The Supreme Court opened the way today for a broad and historic ruling on when, if ever, it is constitutional to impose the death penalty.

In a brief order initialed by Chief Justice Warren E. Burger, the Court agreed to review five murder cases in which death sentences were imposed under statutes enacted following the landmark Supreme Court ruling in 1972 that struck down capital punishment as then practiced in America.

Those statutes, like statutes in more than half the states, were drafted to fit within what legislators perceived as loopholes or possible loopholes in the 1972 ruling.

The five state statutes in today's group of cases are each somewhat different. Together, the five cases — and a sixth death penalty case already before the Court involving a judicial interpretation — appear to represent nearly all the ways that have been devised to date in efforts to draft a capital punishment law that would meet the standards set in the 1972 ruling.

The Supreme Court's action may thus determine whether there is any way for a constitutional law to be written and whether, in the question left undecided by the 1972 case, the death penalty is inherently unconstitutional.

Thirty-four states and the Federal Government now have death penalty laws; a 35th, Illinois, had one as well but a state court recently struck it down as unconstitutional under state law.

As a result of those laws, there are now 411 persons on death row, according to the NAACP Legal Defense and Educational Fund Inc., which is defending many of them.

Nearly all are men; well over half are nonwhite. Their executions have been postponed pending a Supreme Court ruling.

The cases that the court agreed today to review involve six indigent men in all, three white and three black. The states are Louisiana, North Carolina, Florida, Georgia and Texas.

The Louisiana man, Stanislaus Roberts, was convicted of first degree murder as the result of the killing of a gas station attendant during a robbery. The proceeds of the robbery, apparently, were a 38-caliber revolver taken from a desk in the gas station, and $3, which Mr. Roberts's co-defendant obtained when he pumped $3 worth of gasoline into a customer's car and the customer paid.

The North Carolina case, in which two defendants are appealing their death sentences to the Court, also involved a robbery and a shooting. Only one of those defendants, however, Luby Waxton, committed the killing; the second, James Tyrone Woodson, was in a car outside the store at the time. There were also two other co-defendants — one of whom testified at the trial that Mr. Woodson had said earlier on the day of the crime that he "didn't want any part" in the robbery, and that Mr. Waxton had told Mr. Woodson that if the latter didn't come along, he would be killed.

The two other co-defendants pleaded guilty rather than go to trial and thus escaped the death penalty.

In the Florida case, the defendant, Charles William Proffitt, was convicted of killing a man as the man lay sleeping next to the victim's wife in his apartment.

The Georgia defendant is Troy Leon Gregg, who was convicted of the murder and robbery of two men with whom he hitched a ride. Mr. Gregg was sentenced to four death sentences, one for each of the two counts of robbery and two of murder, but the Georgia Supreme Court said that the two sentences on the robbery counts were not imposed in accord with the state law.

In the Texas case, the defendant, Jerry Lane Jerek, 22 years old at the time of the crime, was convicted of murdering a 10-year-old girl after she rebuffed his sexual advances.

The statutes under which each of the men were sentenced to die each include various elements purportedly designed to place stricter controls on the impositions of the penalty, so as to lessen the randomness with which the penalty used to be applied — one of the features of the old system that the Supreme Court faulted in the 1972 case, Furman v. Georgia.

In Louisiana, for example, death is the mandatory sentence for first degree murder. However, Louisiana also has a system of "responsive verdicts," in which the jury can return a verdict of guilty on a lesser offense — thus avoiding the penalty.

North Carolina also has a mandatory sentence for first degree murder (and as well for first degree rape). However, conditions on lesser included offenses are prohibited.

In both Florida and Georgia, there is a "bifurcated" proceeding in which after the trial is held and the defendant convicted, there is a second proceeding to determine sentence, with the jury considering "aggravating" and "mitigating" circumstances. In Florida, the statute explains both types of circumstances: in Georgia, it explains only what is "aggravating."

In Florida, the jury's recommendation is not binding on the judge; in Georgia it is.

The Texas method is something of a hybrid. There is a hearing on sentencing, at which the judge asks the jury to consider three questions: whether the defendant's action was deliberate and was committed with the reasonable expectation death would result; whether there is "probability" that the defendant would commit criminal acts of violence that would threaten society; whether, if the victim provoked the defendant, the defendant's response was unreasonable.

If the jury answers "yes," unanimously, to any of the questions, the judge sentences the defendant to death.

Legislators who drafted such statutes contend that they are legal because while two of the Justices in the five-man majority considered the death penalty inherently cruel and unusual punishment, the other three appeared to base their ruling largely on the fact that judge and juries had uncontrolled discretion and that the penalty ultimately was capriciously imposed on a random few — usually poor and black.

Opponents contend that the penalty is inherently cruel and unusual punishment, and thus unconstitutional.

Death Penalty a 300-Year Issue in America

BY WARREN WEAVER JR. | JULY 3, 1976

On July 2, 1976, the Supreme Court issued a decision in Gregg v. Georgia that reinstated use of the death penalty after a brief moratorium following a 1972 decision against it. The article that follows, published the next day, offers an overview of the history of the death penalty up to that point.

WASHINGTON, JULY 2 — The Supreme Court decision reinstating the death penalty is the latest chapter in a controversy that stretches back more than 300 years into American and Colonial history.

Ever since the 1650's, when colonists could be put to death for denying the true God or cursing their parents, advocates and opponents of capital punishment have clashed almost continuously, in the forum of public opinion, in state legislatures and, most recently, in the courts.

Generally, those seeking to curb or abolish the death penalty gained ground over the years in times of peace and internal security, while proponents of capital punishment advanced their cause in wartime and during periods of national concern over crime and subversion.

CYCLIC HISTORY

Despite its continuous presence as an issue, capital punishment has gone through cycles, with alternating times of activity and success by abolitionists or adherents and long lulls of public indifference in between.

The earliest laws of the American colonies, reflecting their British heritage, were harsh by modern standards but more lenient than those in most of Europe. In Virginia from 1612 through 1619, the death penalty could be imposed for stealing grapes, trading with Indians or killing farm and household animals without permission.

In New York in 1665, the 11 capital crimes included sodomy, kidnapping, traitorous denial of the king's rights and striking a parent, as well as premeditated murder. An earlier Massachusetts code also included adultery, witchcraft and being a rebellious son.

JEFFERSON BILL LOSES

The colonies of Pennsylvania and West Jersey, where Quaker influence was strong, limited the death penalty to treason and willful murder. Rhode Island also had a relatively narrow code.

But elsewhere the prerevolutionary tendency was to increase steadily the number of crimes for which people could be put to death.

The founding of the new nation in 1776 did not rouse any stirrings of reform against the British criminal justice system for some years. A 1785 Virginia bill to limit capital punishment to treason and murder, recommended by a committee headed by Thomas Jefferson, was defeated by one vote in the House of Delegates.

One of the first citizens to advocate publicly the abolition of the death penalty seems to have been Dr. Benjamin Rush, a Philadelphia physician, who in 1787 called the death penalty an "absurd and un-Christian practice."

In 1794 Pennsylvania ended capital punishment except for first-degree murder, and a handful of states reduced the number of capital crimes over the next 20 years.

In the early 19th century, some people began speaking out for abolition, but the chief legislative result was the enactment, in the 1830's, of statutes barring public hanging by Rhode Island, Pennsylvania, New York, Massachusetts and New Jersey, more an issue of taste and order than of conscience.

MORATORIUM IN MAINE

In 1837 Maine became the first state to declare, in effect, a moratorium on capital punishment. The decision was made in part because of riots that had accompanied a public hanging in Augusta.

The Maine law provided that those convicted of capital crimes would spend a year in solitary confinement and would be executed only on order of the governor. The result was no executions.

In the 1840's, abolition of capital punishment became a major public cause, with editors, writers, professional reformers and, above all, clergymen participating. Interestingly, the chief defenders of the death penalty then were more orthodox Protestant clergymen, who relied on Genesis 9:6 — "Whosoever sheddeth a man's blood, so shall his blood be shed."

The abolition leaders attracted attention but won passage of few laws. They played no part in Michigan's 1846 abolition of capital punishment except for the virtually nonexistent crime of treason against the state.

From the beginning of the Mexican War in 1846 through the slavery controversy, the Civil War and its aftermath, there was little activity on the issue, with the nation preoccupied by self-preservation. Early exceptions were successful campaigns to abolish the death penalty in Rhode Island in 1852 and Wisconsin in 1853.

ABOLISHED IN IOWA

From 1870 through 1890, the activity was sporadic, at best. Iowa abolished capital punishment in 1872 and reinstated it six years later. Kansas enacted a law similar to the one Maine had enacted in 1837, and Maine meanwhile approved total abolition.

National interest in the issue was revived when New York adopted electrocution as an instrument of capital punishment and, in 1890, made William Kemmler the first victim of the electric chair. From then until World War I there was a new wave of reform.

In 1897 Congress reduced the number of Federal capital crimes. Then, abolition of the death penalty was voted by Kansas in 1907 and Minnesota in 1911, followed by Washington, North Dakota, South Dakota, Oregon, Arizona and Missouri.

EXECUTION DECLINE

By 1917, twelve states, or a quarter of the nation, had adopted such a ban, and six others had gotten one through at least one house of their legislatures.

The advent of World War I reversed this trend. Rising hatred of foreigners and fear of radicals plus anticipation of a crime wave induced four states to reinstate capital punishment.

Through the Roaring Twenties, the Depression, World War II, the McCarthy era and the Korean War, attempts to abolish the death penalty continued, but with little success beyond the propaganda level.

Still, states executed fewer criminals after World War II than they had before. In 1950 the number was 82 and in 1955 only 76, down from 199 in 1935. The case of Caryl Chessman, who was convicted of kidnapping and spent 12 years on death row before his 1960 execution, attracted wide public attention.

Hawaii and Alaska, not yet states, abolished the death penalty in 1957. So did Delaware in 1958, only to reverse its action in 1961 after some interracial murders. In 1963 New York abandoned the mandatory death sentence for first-degree murder, the last state to do so. Tennessee had begun the shift to a discretionary sentence in 1838.

Abolishing or limiting capital punishment in the 1960's, in addition to New York, were Iowa, Vermont, West Virginia and New Mexico. But referendums with that goal were voted down in Colorado and Massachusetts, and inaction was the general rule.

FOCUS PUT ON COURTS

Then the opponents of the death penalty shifted their attention to the courts, with civil rights lawyers moving into the forefront because of the number of blacks involved.

The NAACP Legal Defense and Educational Fund Inc. began by defending blacks convicted of rape in Southern courts but rapidly expanded their effort. Successful class action suits won stays of execution for all inmates on death row in Florida, then California.

The resulting statistics were startling. There were seven executions in the entire country in 1965, one in 1966, two in 1967. Then they stopped altogether. Meanwhile, the fund's chief trial counsel, Anthony Amsterdam, was bringing lawsuits in an effort to force the courts to declare the death penalty unconstitutional as cruel and unusual punishment.

In two cases, the Supreme Court reversed the convictions of petitioners on other grounds. Finally, in 1972, the Court struck down, by a 5 to 4 vote, the death penalty as then imposed as unconstitutional, setting off attempts by many states to enact new statutes that they hoped would pass legal muster. Today three of the statutes did.

Death Penalty Is Favored

OPINION | BY JOHN F. RUSSO | AUG. 8, 1976

ON JAN. 13 I filed legislation that would reinstate capital punishment in the State of New Jersey. Under my proposed legislation the death penalty would be reinstated for first-degree murder, kidnapping, attempted assassination of the President, Vice President, other heads of government and for treason.

This proposed legislation would meet the United States Supreme Court mandates by providing for a separate sentencing procedure for conviction of capital offenses. For the death penalty to be applicable, the defendant must first be convicted unanimously by a jury and beyond a reasonable doubt of the crimes encompassed. Following such a conviction, the sentencing proceeding would take place before the judge who presided over the trial and before the jury that returned the verdict, or a separate jury, if the circumstances require. The sentencing jury would likewise be required to determine unanimously that the death penalty was warranted before it could take effect.

In the event that the defendant entered a plea of guilty without a jury trial, then the sentencing would be conducted by the judge who accepted the plea and by a specially empanelled jury. The proceeding would be conducted without a jury upon motion of the defendant and with the approval of the court and the state.

The legislation outlines specific aggravating and mitigating factors that can be presented to the jury. And every death sentence would be subject to automatic review by the State Supreme Court.

It should be emphasized that I do not advocate reinstatement of the death penalty in New Jersey with the assumption or hope that it be indiscriminately applied. The standards set forth in the bill, S-639, are quite limiting in their scope and I would not anticipate any large number of convictions with the sentence involving the imposition of capital punishment.

I do not advocate the indiscriminate use of the death penalty. In my own County of Ocean, where I served as prosecutor for 10 years, the death penalty was imposed on only one occasion in the twentieth century. I prosecuted that particular case and recall the traumatic emotional effects upon myself when the death sentence was imposed. I attributed this to a normal reaction that I am sure affects any prosecutor where the extreme penalty is imposed. The imposition of the death penalty would bring no joy to me or any other concerned citizen.

I have long supported the death penalty as a proper method of punishment under appropriate circumstances, although I recognize that serious emotional arguments pro and con will be generated during the debate on this subject. The issue is a profound moral one that is subject to conflicting arguments and philosophical judgments. I can only say that in my judgment capital punishment is warranted.

Many of my opponents refer to the death penalty as the unjustified killing of a human being and suggest perhaps that the "inhumanness" of the state's action should be demonstrated by the televising of an execution. They make a point, but perhaps a point that could be fairly demonstrated only if we were equally able to precede the public execution by a film of the brutal murder that led to it. Of course, such recorded accounts are not available to us and too soon we tend to forget the inhumanity of the murder in our concern over the alleged inhumanness of the imposition of the death penalty.

I support the reinstatement of capital punishment in New Jersey not so much as a deterrent to murder but primarily as a fulfillment of a need and demand of society. Certainly I cannot subscribe to the deterrent value of capital punishment in murders perpetrated by those who act in passion. However, it can hardly be argued that the death penalty is a significant deterrent for carefully contemplated murders such as murders for hire and certainly in cases involving terrorism.

It can be argued, as was done recently by the government in Israel, that it would prevent further acts of terrorism to obtain the release of those imprisoned as a result of offenses involving murder or assassination.

However, the primary function of the death penalty, in my judgment, is particularly well expressed by the opinion of Mr. Justice Stewart of the United States Supreme Court in the recent case of Gregg v. Georgia upholding the death penalty. Justice Stewart stated appropriately:

"In part, capital punishment is an expression of society's moral outrage at particularly offensive conduct. This function may be unappealing to many, but it is essential in an ordered society that asks its citizens to rely on legal processes rather than self help to vindicate their wrongs."

As Justice Stewart pointed out, a large proportion of American society continues to regard the death penalty as an appropriate and necessary sanction. Since the original United States Supreme Court opinion striking down the death penalty, the legislatures of 35 states have enacted new statutes that provide for the death penalty for at least some crimes that result in the death of another person. More recently, the Congress of the United States enacted a statute providing the death penalty for aircraft piracy that results in death.

It should be noted that there have been some suggestions that the death penalty be reinstated only for the death of certain categories of citizens, such as police officers or prison guards. I abhor this view. If the death penalty should be reinstated the imposition of it should not be dependent upon whether or not the victim was wearing a uniform with a badge at the time of his murder.

The death penalty should be available in that case, but also in any type of brutal and aggravated first-degree murder case. I note with interest that this apparently is the view of most police organizations in New Jersey, who feel that the reinstatement of the death penalty, which they support, should not be limited only to the murder of a police officer.

It would be difficult to justify such a limitation upon the death penalty to the parents of a little girl brutally murdered following a sexual attack. No such illusory distinction should be applied.

JOHN F. RUSSO, Democrat of Toms River, is a State Senator.

Backers of the Death Penalty Are Making Scant Progress

BY DOUGLAS KNEELAND | MAY 9, 1977

SAN FRANCISCO, MAY 8 — Legislation to restore the death penalty, despite its current popularity in American public opinion polls, has not been sweeping to victories in all the state legislatures debating the issue.

At the time of the highly publicized execution of Gary Mark Gilmore last Jan. 17 by a Utah firing squad, the first capital punishment administered in the United States in nearly a decade, some vocal opponents of the death penalty predicted a "blood bath." They said that other states would rush to bring their laws into compliance with the Supreme Court's ruling regarding the constitutionality of the death penalty.

But in the nearly four months since the Utah killer was shot, fulfilling his own expressed desire to die rather than serve a life sentence for the two murders he admitted, there have been no further executions. Moreover, the progress of new legislation does not appear to have been speeded up appreciably.

And, while foes of the death penalty have been battling persistently in the courts in a growing number of individual cases to stave off other executions, some of them have taken heart from a few outright legislative victories and from the reluctance with which other states seem to be moving toward the consideration of new statutes.

In the months just before and after the Gilmore execution, attempts to reinstate the death penalty were defeated in the Massachusetts and Kansas legislatures and were killed before floor votes in New Mexico and Hawaii. Opponents are also contending that they stand a good chance of turning back an effort to reinstate the death penalty in Iowa.

"New laws have been passed in many states, but a significant number have not done that," said Deborah Leavy, director of the capital punishment project of the American Civil Liberties Union. "I think that's very encouraging. I think maybe it's beginning to shift. We've been pleased to see that the legislative action has not been a unanimous rush to the death penalty."

Miss Leavy said that she was especially encouraged by the near victory in Nebraska, a generally conservative state where a move to abolish the death penalty failed by one vote.

"I think the very closeness of it shows that not everyone supports the death penalty," she said. "Now that we're talking about real executions, perhaps it won't be so much of a political football. People are showing a little more care. People are thinking about it. If we get them off the high emotional pitch, people are not going to want the death penalty."

David E. Kendall, assistant counsel for the NAACP Legal Defense and Educational Fund Inc., who is deeply involved in his organization's campaign against the death penalty, agreed with her assessment in part.

"The process of legislative revision is going somewhat slowly," he said. "It may be that people now regard the death penalty as available and feel there isn't the need to push it through so fast. Historically, the death penalty has been the sort of punishment people want to have, but not necessarily to implement."

TIME ESTIMATES VIEWED AS WRONG

However, Mr. Kendall was not confident that enough time had elapsed to be certain that the "blood bath" envisioned by some as a result of the Gilmore execution would not yet materialize.

"I always thought people's time estimates on that were wrong," he said. "I think it's coming. I think the fact that there have not been a lot of executions yet by no means means there won't be." The most recent survey in what the civil liberties union calls its "death watch" showed that 27 states now have death penalty laws.

Such legislation in Kentucky, Louisiana, Mississippi, Oklahoma, Tennessee, Virginia and Wyoming was passed in recent months to replace laws struck down as unconstitutional under rulings last summer by the Supreme Court.

In Delaware, Maryland and New Jersey the legislatures have passed laws that have not been signed by the Governors.

Of the remaining 20 that have no current death penalty, the civil liberties union found some sort of legislative action pending in California, Illinois, Iowa, Missouri, North Carolina and South Carolina.

The organization reported that opponents of the bills were expecting victory in Iowa, which abolished the death penalty in 1965. They are also said to have a glimmer of hope in South Carolina, where a strong black caucus in the House has promised to filibuster against the bill.

VOTERS APPROVED DEATH PENALTY

Here in California, a new death penalty bill is moving slowly toward almost certain passage in the Legislature. The new bill, which has been approved by the Senate, was sent by a committee to the floor of the Assembly. But proponents of the bill are not confident that they can muster the two-thirds vote in both houses needed to override a promised veto by Gov. Edmund G. Brown Jr.

In 1972, California voters approved a referendum on the death penalty by a margin of 2 to 1. However, a death penalty bill passed in 1973 was declared unconstitutional by the State Supreme Court last December on the ground that it failed to comply with the United States Supreme Court's rulings of last summer. The state high court said that the statute did not provide for consideration of evidence that might mitigate the death penalty.

The fight to pass a revised law this year has had heavy political overtones. Because of the overwhelming sentiment expressed by voters in 1972, many legislators are reluctant to oppose the bill. And Republicans have made no secret of their intent to use a veto by Governor Brown, a Democrat, as a major issue in their attempts to defeat him in his expected campaign for re-election next year.

Meanwhile, Mr. Kendall of the NAACP fund, which tries to keep a running count of the number of persons facing the death penalty, said that his "best estimate" was that there are now 375 on Death Row.

At the time of the Supreme Court's rulings last July, 588 persons were on Death Row. At last count, death sentences had been set aside for 368 of them in 13 states whose statutes were found to be unconstitutional. However, subsequent death sentences in a number of states have brought the figure up to its present total.

Last July, the Supreme Court upheld the death penalty laws of Florida, Texas and Georgia. In what was considered the milestone case, Gregg v. Georgia, which involved a statute signed into law by then Gov. Jimmy Carter, the Court said, "We hold that the death penalty is not a form of punishment that may never be imposed."

However, it made clear that it preferred a two-step procedure: a trial, then a sentencing hearing at which the jury must consciously choose between life and death.

Despite her guarded optimism that the tide favoring the death penalty may be shifting, Miss Leavy conceded that the civil liberties union and other opponents did not expect to be able to prevent all further executions.

"Somebody's time is going to run out, probably in the next few months," she said. "Our next execution may well be in Georgia. It will be interesting to see if Jimmy Carter wants to make a statement on human rights at that time."

CHAPTER 4

Intellectual Disability and the Death Penalty

When it comes to the question of capital punishment and defendants with intellectual disabilities, public opinion has long favored barring the use of the death penalty. In 2002, the Supreme Court affirmed that the use of the death penalty in such cases was unconstitutional. Yet, since then, states have used varying definitions of intellectual disability and continue to test the limits of that court decision. The following articles shine a light on our developing perspectives on intellectual disability and the death penalty.

Death Penalty Abolished in Bill

BY THE NEW YORK TIMES | APRIL 7, 1914

DISTRICT ATTORNEY WHITMAN has requested a hearing before New York Gov. Glynn on the Blauvelt bills which affect the defense of insanity in criminal cases and the punishment of criminals who plead insanity. According to the District Attorney, the bills substitute in place of the present test of whether the prisoner "knew the nature and quality of his act," a vague and uncertain test which will enable 99 per cent of prisoners to plead irresponsibility.

"One bill," it was said yesterday at the District Attorney's office, "modifies the Code of Criminal Procedure so as to permit a prisoner at his own election to come into court and plead 'guilty, but insane.' The

District Attorney and the court must take the plea. The mere putting in of a plea of 'guilty, but insane' in a murder case requires the court instead of inflicting the death penalty, to sentence the prisoner for life, and in effect abolishes the death penalty at the prisoner's election. It does not say that a prisoner who pleads guilty and is found insane shall be incarcerated for life instead of receiving the death penalty, but the reduction flows automatically from the mere putting in of the plea.

> *Instead of a knowledge of right and wrong, and a realization of his act, being the test of responsibility, the criminal can now say, 'My power to resist was impaired.' 'I suffered from inability to regulate my conduct.' And it should be noted that the extent of the impairment makes no difference. All the accused has to say is, 'I had a slight impairment which prevented me from being able to regulate my conduct.' A man who has a bad temper and lets it go can plead, 'impairment.' A man who covets another's property and steals it can plead that he could not resist — that he was unable to regulate his conduct in that respect. A prisoner would say: 'I was provoked and irritated at the conduct of the man I killed and I couldn't think quite straight at the time, so I killed him.' A bigamist, with an irresistible desire for female society, can escape punishment on the plea that the attractions of the fair sex impaired his ability to regulate his conduct.*

Mr. Whitman has assigned Assistant District Attorney James A. Delehanty to represent his office at a hearing on Thursday before Gov. Glynn on the Fairbank bill, which provides for the release on parole of prisoners who are serving terms for every offense except murder in the first and second degrees. According to Mr. Whitman some 800 prisoners may be released under this law.

In a thirty-two page memorandum, which has been filed with Gov. Glynn, Mr. Whitman says:

> *One of the objects this legislation seeks to accomplish is to make one year the minimum term in practically all sentences, not only those to be hereafter imposed, but those which have already been imposed. The public official who prostitutes and betrays the public trust imposed in him and accepts a bribe to influence his official action, stands on exactly the same*

footing as the imperfectly educated day laborer who, in the moment of passion, strikes another. The bank looter who steals the savings of hundreds is placed on the same footing as the clerk who pilfers the petty cash box. Does this appeal to the public sense of justice and to the public sense of the due execution of penal laws?

The proposed legislation operates practically as a divestiture of a function which from time immemorial has been vested in judicial offices in regard to punishment, and places it almost entirely in the hands of subsidiary agents of the executive branch of the Government? Is this consistent with the spirit of our law and the spirit of our institutions?

Constitution Sometimes Prohibits Executing the Insane, Justices Say

BY STUART TAYLOR JR. | JUNE 27, 1986

THE SUPREME COURT ruled 5 to 4 today that the Constitution bars execution of convicted murderers who have become so insane that they do not know they are about to be killed and the reason for it.

The Court also held that death row prisoners must be given a fair opportunity to establish their insanity, including an impartial officer or board to consider psychiatric presentations and legal arguments made on their behalf.

The Court blocked Florida at least temporarily from executing a man convicted of murder who his attorney says became insane while on death row. The state found him sane enough to be executed, but the Court said Florida's procedures in making that finding had been inadequate.

SOME TESTS ARE CURSORY

The decision also appeared to invalidate procedures in some other states for evaluating such assertions by death row prisoners. No state permits execution of the insane, but states use a variety of procedures, often rather cursory, for testing insanity.

About a dozen of the more than 1,700 inmates on death rows around the nation have had insanity assertions made on their behalf, opponents of the death penalty say. Justice William H. Rehnquist said in dissent that the decision today would create incentives for more.

Justice Thurgood Marshall wrote for the Court. "For centuries no jurisdiction has countenanced the execution of the insane, yet this Court has never decided whether the Constitution forbids the practice," he said. "Today we keep faith with our common-law heritage in holding that it does." Justices Harry A. Blackmun, John Paul Stevens and William J. Brennan Jr. joined his opinion.

POWELL'S VIEW IS CRUCIAL

Justice Lewis F. Powell Jr. joined the portion of Justice Marshall's opinion holding that the Eighth Amendment's ban on "cruel and unusual punishments" prohibits "inflicting the penalty of death upon a prisoner who is insane."

But he said he would not go as far in requiring procedural protections as Justice Marshall, so Justice Powell's opinion apparently represents the holding of the Court on the definition of insanity for purposes of execution and on the procedures required.

Justice Powell said the Constitution barred execution only of those so insane as to be "unaware of the punishment they are about to suffer and why they are to suffer it."

He also said that if the Florida prisoner, Alvin B. Ford, "is cured of his disease, the state is free to execute him." This means that death row inmates who become insane must stay insane to stay alive. The decision today sent Mr. Ford's case back to Federal District Court in Florida to determine if he is sane enough to be executed.

Justice Powell's opinion would go further in protecting Mr. Ford than would Chief Justice Warren E. Burger and Justices William H. Rehnquist, Sandra Day O'Connor and Byron R. White, who said the Constitution does not bar execution of the insane.

Justices O'Connor and White sided with Mr. Ford, but not on the central constitutional issue. They said instead that Florida's procedures violated due process of the law because they did not provide even "minimal procedural protections" for Mr. Ford's right under Florida law not to be executed while insane.

REHNQUIST DISSENTS

Justice Rehnquist filed a dissent, which was joined by Chief Justice Burger.

Justice Rehnquist said that "creating a constitutional right to a judicial determination of sanity" offered "an invitation to those who have nothing to lose by accepting it to advance entirely spurious claims of insanity."

"A prisoner found sane two days before execution might claim to have lost his sanity the next day, thus necessitating another judicial determination of his sanity and presumably another stay of his execution," he added.

The issue in the case, Ford v. Wainwright, No. 85-5542, was unrelated to the defense raised by some prisoners at their trials that they are not responsible for their crimes because they were insane at the time they committed them.

Mr. Ford did not say he had been insane in 1974 when he killed a Fort Lauderdale police officer while robbing a restaurant. He was convicted of murder and sentenced to die that year. His lawyer, Richard Burr, and his psychiatrist argued that he had gradually gone mad in 1982 and 1983 while on death row at the Florida State Prison in Starke.

SERIES OF DELUSIONS

They said he had had a succession of delusions, including that he was "Pope John Paul III." They also said he sometimes lapsed into complete incomprehensibility.

When Mr. Ford's lawyer asserted he could not be executed because he was insane, Gov. Bob Graham appointed a panel of three psychiatrists, who interviewed Mr. Ford for about 30 minutes. While two of the doctors diagnosed him as psychotic, all three agreed that he understood why he was to die, as required by state law.

The Governor, while refusing to consider the reports of two other psychiatrists submitted by Mr. Ford's lawyer, signed Mr. Ford's death warrant April 30, 1984, without explanation.

Justice Marshall noted today that for centuries the common law had condemned execution of the insane as "savage and inhuman" and that "no state in the Union permits the execution of the insane."

"Today, no less than before," he said, "we may seriously question the retributive value of executing a person who has no comprehension of why he has been singled out and stripped of his fundamental right to life."

Justice Marshall also cited "the natural abhorrence civilized societies feel at killing one who has no capacity to come to grips with his own conscience or Deity" and the need "to protect the dignity of society itself from the barbarity of exacting mindless vengeance."

Justices Marshall and Powell both said Florida's procedures violated due process because they did not guarantee Mr. Ford's lawyer an opportunity to submit evidence or arguments on his behalf and placed the decision "wholly within the executive branch," under a Governor who was also "the commander of the state's corps of prosecutors."

Citing 'National Consensus,' Justices Bar Death Penalty for Retarded Defendants

BY LINDA GREENHOUSE | JUNE 21, 2002

THE CONSTITUTION BARS the execution of mentally retarded offenders, the Supreme Court declared today in a landmark death penalty ruling based on the majority's view that a "national consensus" now rejected such executions as excessive and inappropriate.

Of the 38 states that have a death penalty, 18 now prohibit executing the retarded, up from 2 when the court last considered the question in 1989. This "dramatic shift in the state legislative landscape," especially when anticrime legislation is extremely popular, "provides powerful evidence that today our society views mentally retarded offenders as categorically less culpable than the average criminal," Justice John Paul Stevens wrote for the 6-to-3 majority.

The decision, in the case of a Virginia man with an I.Q. of 59 who was convicted of committing a murder and robbery at the age of 18, could ultimately move 200 or more people off death row. Mental health experts believe that as many as 10 percent of those convicted of capital murder are mentally retarded, although states often dispute the claim in individual cases.

In fact, Virginia is disputing the evidence that the defendant in this case, Daryl R. Atkins, is retarded. The Supreme Court said today that it would be up to the states to develop "appropriate ways" to apply the new constitutional prohibition. The generally accepted definition of mental retardation is an I.Q. of approximately 70 or less accompanied by limitations on abilities like communication or caring for oneself.

The dissenters today, Chief Justice William H. Rehnquist and Justices Antonin Scalia and Clarence Thomas, disputed that there was a real or lasting consensus against executing the retarded. In a dissenting opinion that he read from the bench, Justice Scalia said that 18 states out of 38 was only 47 percent, not even half.

In the absence of an authentic consensus, the majority had simply enshrined its own views as constitutional law, he said, adding, "The arrogance of this assumption of power takes one's breath away."

Further, he said, "there is something to be said for popular abolition of the death penalty; there is nothing to be said for its incremental abolition by this court."

Chief Justice Rehnquist said the majority had improperly gone beyond looking at state legislative action to consider polling data and international opinion as well. "If it is evidence of a national consensus for which we are looking, then the viewpoints of other countries simply are not relevant," he said.

The 15 countries of the European Union filed a brief on behalf of Mr. Atkins, as did a group of senior American diplomats who told the court that the practice of executing retarded offenders was out of step with much of the world and was a source of friction between the United States and other countries.

Amnesty International said that since 1995, only three countries were reported to have executed mentally retarded people: Kyrgyzstan, Japan and the United States, which the organization said had executed 35 mentally retarded defendants since the court allowed states to reinstate the death penalty in 1976. The court's decision today "will provide the U.S. criminal justice system with a critical tool to uphold human rights standards," the organization said.

The decision overturns a ruling of the Virginia Supreme Court.

While the justices disputed the outcome, there was no dispute on the basic analytic approach, unique to the Eighth Amendment, that depends on a sense of community norms to decide whether a practice violates the prohibition against cruel and unusual punishment. All agreed with the statement of Chief Justice Earl Warren in a 1958 case, Trop v. Dulles, that "the amendment must draw its meaning from the evolving standards of decency that mark the progress of a maturing society." Rather, the debate was over whether the evidence supported the evolution that the majority discerned.

The court's previous examination of the retardation question came in 1989 in a Texas case, Penry v. Lynaugh, in which Justice Sandra Day O'Connor's controlling opinion said that there was no current consensus against executing the retarded but kept the court's door open to future developments.

The developments came quickly. From the original two states, Georgia and Maryland, the list of states exempting retarded people from capital punishment grew to include New Mexico, Kentucky, Tennessee, Arkansas, Colorado, Washington, Indiana, Kansas, Nebraska, South Dakota, Arizona, Connecticut, Florida, Missouri and New York, which excluded the retarded when it reinstated its death penalty in 1995. The federal death penalty, reinstated in 1988, exempted the retarded.

When the court agreed last year to revisit the issue, it did so in a case from North Carolina, but North Carolina abolished the death penalty for the retarded last summer, before that case, McCarver v. North Carolina, No. 00-8727, could be argued. The justices then substituted the case they decided today, Atkins v. Virginia, No. 00-8452. It appeared earlier this year that the Atkins case might become moot as well. In February, the Virginia State Senate voted unanimously to abolish capital punishment for the retarded, but the House decided to delay action until after the Supreme Court decision.

Surveying this rapidly changing landscape, Justice Stevens noted that the numbers alone did not tell the full story.

"It is not so much the number of these states that is significant, but the consistency of the direction of change," especially in a strong anticrime climate, he said.

Even most states that nominally allow executing the retarded were not actually carrying out such executions, Justice Stevens said, concluding, "The practice, therefore, has become truly unusual, and it is fair to say that a national consensus has developed against it."

SHELLY KATZ/THE LIFE IMAGES COLLECTION/GETTY IMAGES

Mentally retarded death row inmate Johnny Paul Penry sitting in his cell in 1989. Mr. Penry was convicted for charges of rape and murder.

The opinion, joined by Justices O'Connor, Anthony M. Kennedy, David H. Souter, Ruth Bader Ginsburg and Stephen G. Breyer, did not end there. Justice Stevens went on to consider whether there was any reason the court should disregard or disagree with the legislative judgments. He concluded that, to the contrary, the state judgments were supported by a review of various factors making the death penalty particularly inappropriate for retarded defendants.

"Some characteristics of mental retardation undermine the strength of the procedural protections that our capital jurisprudence steadfastly guards," Justice Stevens said, adding that as a result, "mentally retarded defendants in the aggregate face a special risk of wrongful execution."

Among the factors he cited were their "diminished capacities to understand and process information" and to reason logically and control impulses. These characteristics do not mean that retarded defendants who are competent to stand trial should not face criminal punishment, Justice Stevens said, "but they do diminish their personal culpability" and indicate that the usual justifications for capital punishment, retribution and deterrence, are less applicable than to defendants with normal intelligence.

This part of the opinion might have broader significance for the court's death penalty jurisprudence, said one death penalty expert, Professor Michael Mello of Vermont Law School.

"It shows that a majority of the court is willing to take a fresh look at the real capital punishment, how the system really works," said Professor Mello, a former defense lawyer who opposes the death penalty.

He predicted that the court might be open to revisiting precedents that make it all but impossible for appellate courts to consider assertions of actual innocence if the defendant has not followed exacting procedures.

None of the current members of the court hold a position in flat opposition to the death penalty.

Neither the majority nor the dissenters discussed the retroactive implications of the decision. Under the court's constitutional jurisprudence, the decision applies retroactively as a general matter, but states could raise objections to granting relief to defendants who had not argued the retardation issue in earlier appeals. If the lower federal courts disagree on how such cases should be handled, the question could conceivably come back to the Supreme Court, where a majority appears ready to grant full retroactivity.

Last Chance for Warren Hill

EDITORIAL | BY THE NEW YORK TIMES | JULY 11, 2013

The case of Warren Hill drew international attention, as four doctors found Hill to have an intellectual disability, yet the State of Georgia pushed forward with plans to execute him, claiming he did not meet the state's uniquely high standard for defining intellectual disability. On Jan. 27, 2015, the Supreme Court declined to grant a stay of execution, and Hill was executed that same day.

JUSTICE HARRY BLACKMUN surely would have confronted the case of Warren Lee Hill Jr. — whom the state of Georgia plans to execute Monday evening — by recalling perhaps his most famous dissent. "From this day forward," he wrote in a 1994 Supreme Court case, "I no longer shall tinker with the machinery of death."

Mr. Hill was already serving a life sentence for the murder of his girlfriend when, in 1990, he bludgeoned another inmate to death with a nail-studded board. He was tried and sentenced to death. He subsequently claimed that he was mentally retarded and could not be executed under Georgia law.

Four experts testified that Mr. Hill met the generally accepted criteria for mild mental retardation. Three others said he did not for various reasons, one being that he had served in the Navy. Georgia, alone among the states, requires that mental retardation be proved beyond a reasonable doubt, the strictest standard in our justice system. The federal courts in Georgia ruled that Mr. Hill had not met this standard.

But, in the past year, the three state experts all voluntarily recanted their testimony. It didn't matter: the wheels of the machinery of death in Georgia keep turning, greased by a breathtakingly strict federal law meant to prevent prisoners from filing multiple appeals, even if those appeals contain crucial new evidence. Under this law, every avenue to Mr. Hill is now blocked save one: a direct appeal to the Supreme Court, which his lawyers filed this week.

In 2002, the court ruled that mentally retarded people may not be executed. All seven experts who have examined Mr. Hill now agree he is mentally retarded. If that doesn't count as proof beyond a reasonable doubt, it is hard to imagine what would.

Florida's Unconstitutional Death Penalty

EDITORIAL | BY THE NEW YORK TIMES | MARCH 3, 2014

AS THE DEATH PENALTY becomes rarer and more concentrated in a few parts of the country, the states that continue to employ it are resorting to more desperate schemes to kill people.

In January, for the third time in as many months, Missouri executed an inmate whose appeals were still pending. (A federal appellate judge wrote that he was "alarmed" by the state's conduct.) Meanwhile, several states are refusing to disclose where they are buying the execution drugs they use, which come from unregulated compounding pharmacies.

And while the Supreme Court categorically banned the execution of people with intellectual disabilities as unconstitutional in 2002, some states continue to defy that principle by interpreting the court's words as narrowly as possible. In that case, Atkins v. Virginia, the court said reduced mental capacity made a defendant less culpable, but left it to states to enforce the ruling.

On Monday, the court heard oral arguments in a case challenging Florida's attempt to get around the 2002 decision by requiring intellectual disability to be proved by an I.Q. score of 70 or less, even though the test includes a margin of error of five points.

The defendant, Freddie Lee Hall, was sentenced to death in 1978 for murdering a pregnant woman named Karol Hurst. Over the years, Mr. Hall has scored between 69 and 80 on I.Q. tests. In 1991, a Florida court heard expert testimony and found that Mr. Hall has been "mentally retarded his entire life," but upheld his sentence because capital punishment was not yet prohibited in such cases. After the 2002 Atkins decision, Mr. Hall seemed to have a strong case that he was ineligible for execution. Yet Florida kept him on death row because he had I.Q. scores higher than 70. This reasoning runs counter to the consensus among mental-health professionals, who see I.Q. tests as approximate, incomplete measures and reject strict cutoffs in reading the results.

It also goes against the Supreme Court's ruling, which relied on a multipronged clinical definition of intellectual disability that considers limitations in adaptive functioning, like interpersonal skills and self-care. Under Florida's law, none of that matters if a defendant scores higher than 70.

Several justices appeared skeptical of that rigid approach. "Your rule prevents us from getting a better understanding of whether that I.Q. score is accurate or not," Justice Anthony Kennedy told the state's attorney. "We cannot even reach the adaptive functioning prong."

Justice Elena Kagan asked why Florida refuses to consider the margin of error, even though state officials don't dispute that it is part of any test-score interpretation. The lawyer for the state responded that using accepted scientific practice "would double the number of people who are eligible" to be exempt from execution. "And that's inconsistent with Florida's purposes," he said.

Florida's purpose, in other words, is not to comply with the Supreme Court's ruling, but to execute its death-row inmates whether or not they are intellectually disabled. The court rejected that practice once. It should do so again, unequivocally, for those states that missed the message the first time.

Court Extends Curbs on the Death Penalty in a Florida Ruling

BY ADAM LIPTAK | MAY 27, 2014

WASHINGTON — The Supreme Court on Tuesday continued a trend to limit capital punishment, ruling that Florida's I.Q. score cutoff was too rigid to decide which mentally disabled individuals must be spared the death penalty.

"Florida seeks to execute a man because he scored a 71 instead of 70 on an I.Q. test," Justice Anthony M. Kennedy wrote for the majority in a 5-to-4 decision.

Justice Kennedy was joined by the court's four-member liberal wing, a recurring coalition in cases concerning harsh punishments.

When the court barred the execution of people with mental disabilities in 2002 in Atkins v. Virginia, it largely let the states determine who qualified. Tuesday's decision, Justice Samuel A. Alito Jr. wrote for the four dissenters, represented a "sea change" in the court's approach.

The ruling will affect not only Florida, which has the nation's second-largest death row after California, but also as many as eight other states by Justice Kennedy's count, including Alabama and Virginia. They will now be required to take a less mechanical approach to mental disability in capital cases, said Eric M. Freedman, a law professor at Hofstra.

"Death row inmates commonly suffer from multidimensional mental problems," Mr. Freedman said. "Today's ruling requires courts to investigate these fully, by looking at the elephant rather than the tail."

In Tuesday's decision, Justice Kennedy said that closer supervision of the states was warranted given the nature of the punishment. "The death penalty is the gravest sentence our society may impose," he wrote. "Persons facing that most severe sanction must have a fair opportunity to show that the Constitution prohibits their execution. Florida's law contravenes our nation's commitment to dignity and its duty to teach human decency as the mark of a civilized world."

The case, Hall v. Florida, No. 12-10882, arose from the 1978 murder of Karol Hurst, who was 21 and seven months pregnant when Freddie L. Hall and an accomplice forced her into her car in a supermarket parking lot. She was found in a wooded area, where she had been beaten, sexually assaulted and shot.

There was significant evidence in school and court records of Mr. Hall's intellectual disability. Before the Supreme Court's decision in the Atkins case, a trial judge found that there was "substantial evidence" that Mr. Hall "has been mentally retarded his entire life."

After the Atkins decision, Mr. Hall challenged his death sentence, relying in part on the earlier state court determinations.

The Atkins decision gave states only general guidance. It said a finding of intellectual disability required proof of three things: "subaverage intellectual functioning," meaning low I.Q. scores; a lack of fundamental social and practical skills; and the presence of both conditions before age 18. The court said I.Q. scores under "approximately 70" typically indicate disability.

A Florida law enacted not long before the Atkins decision created what Mr. Hall's lawyers called an "inflexible bright-line cutoff" requiring proof of an I.Q. of 70 or below.

In 2012, the Florida Supreme Court ruled that Mr. Hall was eligible to be executed because his I.Q. had been measured at various times as 71, 73 and 80.

That approach, Justice Kennedy wrote, had at least two flaws. One was that it failed to take account of standard errors of measurement.

"An individual's score is best understood as a range of scores on either side of the recorded score," he wrote.

The second problem, he said, was that a rigid cutoff excludes consideration of other evidence. "Intellectual disability is a condition, not a number," he wrote.

Justice Alito protested that this changed the rules announced in Atkins, which required both low scores and more practical proof. He was also sharply critical of the court's reliance on the views of medical experts, saying the majority had overruled part of the Atkins decision "based largely on the positions adopted by private professional organizations."

The Supreme Court assesses whether given practices are barred by the Eighth Amendment's prohibition of cruel and unusual punishment by considering, in the words of a 1958 decision, "the evolving standards of decency that mark the progress of a maturing society."

In doing so, Justice Alito said, it had always "meant the standards of American society as a whole."

"Now, however," he wrote, "the court strikes down a state law based on the evolving standards of professional societies, most notably the American Psychiatric Association."

Chief Justice John G. Roberts Jr. and Justices Antonin Scalia and Clarence Thomas joined the dissent.

The majority and dissenting opinions clashed over statistics and over how many states had laws similar to Florida's. By Justice Kennedy's count, Kentucky and Virginia have adopted a fixed cutoff of 70 by statute, and Alabama by court decision.

Five other states (Arizona, Delaware, Kansas, North Carolina and Washington), Justice Kennedy said, have laws open to the same interpretation.

Justices Ruth Bader Ginsburg, Stephen G. Breyer, Sonia Sotomayor and Elena Kagan joined the majority opinion. In earlier decisions limiting the use of the death penalty and other harsh punishments under the Eighth Amendment, Justice Kennedy has often joined the court's liberal wing. He wrote several of those decisions, sometimes using the soaring language that marked his majority opinion on Tuesday.

"The Eighth Amendment's protection of dignity," he wrote, "reflects the nation we have been, the nation we are, and the nation we aspire to be. This is to affirm that the nation's constant, unyielding purpose must be to transmit the Constitution so that its precepts and guarantees retain their meaning and force."

Justice Kennedy was also in the majority in cases striking down the death penalty for the mentally disabled, for juvenile offenders and for non-homicide crimes and in ones limiting the use of life without parole sentences for juvenile offenders.

The court returned Mr. Hall's case to the lower courts for a fresh assessment of his condition. "Freddie Lee Hall may or may not be intellectually disabled," Justice Kennedy wrote, "but the law requires that he have the opportunity to present evidence of his intellectual disability, including deficits in adaptive functioning over his lifetime."

CHAPTER 5

Juvenile Offenders and the Death Penalty

While it is now accepted that the execution of an offender who committed a crime as a juvenile is unconstitutional, it was not always so. Between 1976 and 2005, 226 juvenile offenders were sentenced to the death penalty, and 22 of them were executed. As recently as 1989, the Supreme Court upheld the legality of such executions. However, in tune with public opinion, the Court reversed its stance in the 2005 case Roper v. Simmons. Following are a selection of articles on the death penalty and juvenile offenders.

Boy, 17, Will Face Second Execution

BY LEWIS WOOD | JAN. 14, 1947

WASHINGTON, JAN. 13 — By the narrow division of five to four the Supreme Court ruled today that Louisiana may lawfully order another execution for Willie Francis, the 17-year-old slayer who escaped death when the electric chair failed to operate.

In this case, which the high tribunal declared "without precedent in any court," the majority included Chief Justice Fred M. Vinson and Justices Hugo L. Black, Stanley F. Reed, Robert H. Jackson and Felix Frankfurter.

The author of the majority opinion was Mr. Reed, who held that Francis would not be subjected to the double jeopardy of cruel and unusual punishments barred by the Constitution, nor denied the equal protection of the laws. In a concurrence, Mr. Frankfurter held that Louisiana was quite within her legal rights.

WOULD REMAND CASE

For the minority, Justice Harold H. Burton demanded that the case be returned to the Louisiana Supreme Court, where all the circumstances would be examined and especially whether Francis had the right to be executed by a "continuous" stream of electricity, rather than by "repeated" efforts. Also in minority were Justices William O. Douglas, Frank Murphy and Wiley Rutledge.

Francis, convicted of the murder of Andrew Thomas, in a holdup where Thomas was robbed of $4 and his watch, was strapped in Louisiana's portable electric chair last May. But when the electric switch was thrown, "presumably because of some mechanical difficulty, death did not result."

He was taken from the chair and sent back to prison. A new death warrant was issued, fixing the execution for May 9, but a stay was obtained while the boy's case was argued in the courts. The Louisiana Supreme Court ruled against Francis and his case was argued in the Supreme Court at Washington Nov. 18 last. Louisiana dispatches say that Governor Davis will set another execution date when the Supreme Court's formal papers arrive.

For the majority, Justice Reed said that "we see no difference from the constitutional point of view between a new trial for an error of law at the instance of the State that results in a death sentence instead of imprisonment for life and an execution that follows failure of equipment."

ACCIDENT IS DISCUSSED

"When an accident, with no suggestion of malevolence," he continued, "prevents the consummation of the sentence, the State's subsequent course in the administration of its criminal law is not affected on that account by any requirement of due process of law, under the Fourteenth Amendment (of the Federal Constitution). We find no double jeopardy here which can be said to amount to a denial of Federal due process in the proposed execution."

The majority, Justice Reed went on, could also find nothing in what had transpired "which amounts to cruel and unusual punishment in the constitutional sense."

"Even the fact that (Francis) has already been subjected to a current of electricity does not make his subsequent execution any more cruel in the constitutional sense than any other execution," he said. "The cruelty against which the Constitution protects a convicted man is cruelty inherent in the method of punishment, not the necessary suffering involved in any method employed to extinguish life humanely."

Justice Frankfurter, in his concurrence, said the Supreme Court (except in extreme circumstances) must refrain from interfering with State action, no matter "how strong one's personal feeling of revulsion against a State's insistence on its pound of flesh."

Justice Burton, in his dissent, termed it "unthinkable" that any State would pass a law authorizing capital punishment by "repeated applications of an electric current separated by intervals of days or hours until finally death shall result."

He conceded that Louisiana had not done this; and noted, on the other hand, that her law prescribed "continuance of such current through the body of the person convicted until such person is dead." And then he commented:

> *If the State officials deliberately and intentionally had placed (Francis) in the electric chair five times and applied electric current to his body in a manner not sufficient, until the final time, to kill him, such a form of torture would rival that of burning at the stake. How many deliberate and intentional reapplications of electric current does it take to produce a cruel, unusual and unconstitutional punishment?*

Too Young to Die?

BY RON ROSENBAUM | MARCH 12, 1989

"I WAS SCARED. I knew something was gonna happen," Heath Wilkins recalls. "My life had become unbearable to me. It was the first time I was out on my own, the first time nobody was responsible for me — see what I'm saying?"

We're in a holding cell in the Clay County Detention Center, down the block from the Jesse James Bank Museum in Liberty, Mo. Heath Wilkins is describing his state of mind in 1985, when he was 16 years old, sleeping in a kiddie park and about to commit the murder that would send him to death row.

That murder — even more, that state of mind — will be at the heart of the matter on March 27 when the Supreme Court takes up Wilkins v. Missouri (in tandem with Stanford v. Kentucky) and begins to decide whether up to 27 juvenile murderers in American prisons will live or die.

Last June, in Thompson v. Oklahoma, the Court narrowly ruled against the execution of William Wayne Thompson, who was 15 years old at the time of his crime, in effect making 16 the minimum age for execution in the United States. The next day, the Court agreed to consider the Wilkins case, and by extension, whether it would spare 16-year-old offenders as well. But the closely divided plurality in the Thompson case left in doubt the Court's future direction in the "juvenile death penalty" cases which now constitute the cutting edge of capital punishment litigation.

What the debate comes down to is the enigma of the adolescent mind, specifically of adolescent moral development. Do juveniles have the moral autonomy to be "depraved," the way the worst adult killers are said to be "knowingly depraved"? How old *does* one have to be to be capable of conscious evil?

Heath Wilkins, who is now 20, is something of an enigma himself. In fact, he reveals himself, in a four-hour jail-cell interview, to be almost as deeply divided as the courts on the question of whether he should die.

Shortly after pleading guilty to the 1985 stabbing of Nancy Allen, a 27-year-old mother of two, in the course of a liquor store robbery in Avondale, Mo., Wilkins "fired" his public defender and, in a bizarre penalty-phase hearing, tried to call witnesses to prosecute the case *for* the death penalty against himself. If his choice was between the horror of lifetime confinement and death by execution, he told the court, he'd take death because "one I fear, the other I don't." On June 27, 1986, a Clay County judge sentenced Wilkins to the fate he sought. Then, a year and a half later, at the last moment, he had a change of heart and signed on to the state public defender's Supreme Court appeal of his death sentence.

Even now, he says, he doesn't feel justified in pleading for his life. "In my opinion, I got what I deserved," he told me. "I would like a chance, but I don't think I can ask for it. In a way, that makes all this [the Supreme Court appeal] easier to deal with, see what I'm saying? It's better than the situation in Soviet prisons. They're innocent."

Here in the narrow holding cell, there are moments when Wilkins, who is not in leg irons during this interview, could pass, on the surface, for a typically restless, gawky American adolescent of the non-Satanist heavy-metal, good-old-boy subspecies. The kind of kid you might see wearing a feed-lot gimme-cap to a Rush concert at the Speedway.

But there are many more ways in which he is neither a typical teenager nor a typical "teen killer." He's probably the only active Smithsonian member on Death Row; he uses his membership discount to send off for aeronautics books in Air and Space/Smithsonian magazine. In his cell, he designs what he describes as improvements on "twin-propeller drive systems" for ultralight aircraft. He reads 20th-century Russian novelists and on occasion displays a bitter, satiric way with words of his own. He calls the mental-health counselors in juvenile institutions "the mental machines of society" and claims he learned to fool them by "playing" their therapy game "like Stalin played socialism."

Searching for the right combination of words to express his complicated thoughts on contrition and punishment, he'll lean forward, narrowing his eyes, and punctuate almost everything he says with the addition or interjection of, "See what I'm saying?"

Habitual as this is, it seems to reflect a real urgency to be understood. A psychiatrist at the Menninger Clinic in Topeka, Kan., picked up on this urgency in poems the boy had written and came up with a striking image to describe it. He called it "a form of reparation for his own sense of badness ... analogous to the current program of telecasting radio messages into outer space in the hope, against all odds, that a distant being will hear and understand the message."

And so, while Wilkins isn't sure he wants to save his life, he is willing to attempt to explain it. With his account, and with corroborative material from court files and interviews, it's possible to re-create his state of mind at the time of his crime, the state of mind the Supreme Court will be addressing, the one that drove Heath Wilkins in his final weeks of freedom direct from a children's playground to death row.

On Aug. 2, 1985, an undercover informant told the Kansas City Police metro squad he had information on the murder of Nancy Allen six days earlier.

The kids responsible, the informer said, were hanging out in Penguin Park. Ron Nicola, a metro squad detective, recalls the peculiar way the report sounded when it came in: "He said there's a bunch of cement animals and stuff there in Penguin Park and [the suspects] were living in the kangaroo."

Penguin Park is a one-acre piece of scrubby grass in Kansas City, dominated by three-story-high cement statues of cartoonish animals. There's the jolly-looking, eponymous penguin and next to it, the enormous mamma kangaroo, resting a protective maternal paw on a wide-eyed baby kangaroo gazing apprehensively out at the world from the security of the 10-foot-high marsupial pouch.

In his holding cell, Heath Wilkins stares at a Polaroid taken at the park.

"Yeah, this is where we lived, right in here," he says, pointing to the pouch of the kangaroo. "We never slept in the penguin. It smelled."

He explains the sleeping arrangements: "I slept here," he says, pointing to the packed dirt base at the bottom of the pouch, "and Midget, my girlfriend, would sleep up on the top next to the baby. You know, you can lie down there."

It was only the third time he'd been in love, he says. He met her when they were both in juvenile detention. Called her up as soon as they were both out.

"I'm not the kind to just — I only went with girlfriends I'd fallen in love with," he says. "I'm a real classical character like that."

He had no home to go to; she had a home but didn't want to be there. She'd left it taking $800 with her, which paid for a cheap motel room for the two of them for about a month.

When the money ran out and they had no place to sleep but the kangaroo, the two of them talked of somehow getting out to California. There was even a report in a prosecution file that they'd gone window shopping for wedding rings.

"Yeah," he says softly, when asked about it. "Yeah. Yeah. Forgot about that. Huh." He shakes his head. "In Helzberg's jewelers, at the mall."

It wasn't much of a life they had together. Heath and Midget spent their days at the Antioch Shopping Center, scrounging for food with a couple of other homeless teen-agers who went by the streets names Bo and Shades. Someone would shoplift some slices from Show Biz Pizza; they'd play some Robotron at the video arcade. At night, they'd drift back to nearby Sherwood lake. Someone would shoplift some cigarettes, maybe a bottle of peach schnapps, from Linda's Liquors. Then they'd go down by the lake, drink, smoke, maybe trip out on "black dragon," a homemade drug Wilkins said was LSD.

Heath Wilkins liked black dragon. When he took it, he once told a psychiatrist, "he could see the individual molecules of things." It "caused sound to be turned into liquid that would pour through his head, through his ears." And "when he closed his eyes, he could imagine anything."

When he opened them, however, the reality was that things were closing in on him. He knew "something scary was coming," Wilkins told me.

What he recalls most about the days leading up to the crime, he says, is "how hungry we were all the time ... , I was *starved*. We were down to looking for money in the dirt on the side of the road."

It was his first time on his own. He'd been under the supervision of juvenile authorities since the age of 8, after he'd apparently attempted to poison one of his mother's boyfriends, who, he claimed, had beaten and terrorized him. Two years later, he was removed from his mother's custody, and subsequent petty crimes kept him incarcerated most of the rest of his life. He'd hated confinement, but now that he was free he was "scared all the time."

At the core of his panic was his realization that "nobody was responsible for me any more." His only official guardians were the juvenile authorities, but they'd lost track of him.

Court records make it possible to pinpoint the moment when a stitch was dropped in the social safety net and Heath Wilkins fell through. It happened one month before the murder, when Wilkins "freaked out and acted crazy," ranting and raving, in order, he says now, to get himself kicked out of a Job Corps camp in Clearview, Utah.

The Job Corps stint was supposed to be a fulfillment of a juvenile probation period for a burglary Heath had committed at age 15. When the Job Corps put him on a plane back to Kansas City, the juvenile authorities released him to the custody of his mother. But his mother, a credit card company employee, refused to let him stay with her. He'd always been too much trouble, and anyway, he was the state's responsibility. (Since Wilkins's death sentence, he and his mother have reconciled.)

The juvenile authorities were only belatedly made aware that Wilkins was homeless. A notation in the files mentions reports that Wilkins — who'd been diagnosed as having "suicidal" and "homicidal" tendencies at age 10 — was living "on the streets." Follow-up was recommended — but by then it was too late.

Heath's tale of his attempts to live on his own in the month before the murder is one episode after another of rejection, eviction and humiliation. For a few days after he got back from Utah, Heath slept in the back seat of a trashed-out car parked in front of a friend's place a few doors down from his mother's home. But the friend evicted him from the junk heap, "because it didn't look good. It was politics before friendship, see what I'm saying?"

Then another "friend" who had given him a place to stay confiscated his wages from a part-time ditch-digging job as "back rent" and evicted him. Then there was a convoluted dispute with a tree-trimmer over wages at another job, which ended, Wilkins says, when the tree-trimmer threatened his life.

"I thought he was going to come after me, kill me. That's when I went to Penguin Park. Had no place else to go."

He saw no way out of the kangaroo. Except one vague, slim hope in the form of a broken motorcycle.

"Some guy I knew had a bike, a 750 that was busted. I figured if I could buy it, I could fix it up, head down to Arkansas." In Arkansas he thought he could look for the father he hadn't seen since he was 5. To execute this escape plan, though, he'd first have to find a way to buy the busted 750.

The single ground rule of my interview with Wilkins, insisted on by his public defender, Sean O'Brien, was that Wilkins wouldn't talk about the actual commission of the crime.

The facts of the matter, however, are simple: On the night of July 27, 1985, Heath, his girlfriend Midget and their friends Bo and Shades planned to carry out a robbery. "It was my plan," Heath told me. "Every decision." He had chosen the objective, the cottage-like building called Linda's Liquors.

Heath and Bo arrived there shortly before 11. Heath ordered a sandwich. Bo hid in the bathroom. Heath asked for extra lettuce. When the woman in the store turned her back, Bo emerged from hiding. And Heath pulled a knife.

Nancy Allen's husband, David, was on duty that night at the North Kansas City Bureau of Investigation. It's really just a private security firm with an official-sounding name, but it provided services to Linda's Liquors and Deli, a little bottle and sandwich shop. David and Nancy Allen were a young couple struggling to raise two kids in a declining, blue-collar neighborhood of North Kansas City. David's brother, Robert Allen, thinking the extra income would help out, had offered Nancy a job at Linda's Liquors, which he co-owned. It was the night shift, and she'd be alone in the place, but her husband would be watching over her from the nearby North Kansas City Bureau of Investigation. Indeed, every night around midnight, when Nancy would lock up and prepare to leave, she'd flip a switch in Linda's Liquors and a signal light would go on at N.K.C.B.I., indicating everything was O.K. and the alarms were set for the night.

That night, the light didn't come on at 12. When David tried to call his wife, no one picked up the phone. He ordered one of the N.K.C.B.I. patrol cars over to Linda's Liquors. He called 911. On the phone tape, his voice can be heard, full of dread, urging the police to "hurry, it's my wife!"

Larry Harman wants Heath Wilkins to die. It was Harman who, as Clay County prosecutor in 1985, went to Linda's Liquors that night in time to see the body when the eight bloody stab wounds were still fresh. And it was Harman who, at the sentencing hearing in 1986 — the one in which Wilkins made the case for his own death — made the crucial decision to throw the weight of the state behind the teenager's death wish.

Harman still thinks Heath Wilkins deserves to be executed, and to prove it, takes me on a tour. He takes me to the kiddie-park kangaroo where the murder was planned and tells me that because of Wilkins's youth, he "struggled" with the decision to ask for death, says he didn't finally decide "until the very, very last moment" to ask the judge for it. ("Yes, he was young," Harman told the sentencing hearing. "But the victim was young.") He takes me to the Clay County sheriff's office, shows me police photos of the body, points out the stab wounds in the neck and reminds me that after Wilkins stabbed Nancy Allen in the back, the chest and the heart, he then stabbed her in the throat four times, "to silence her pleading for her life."

And then back at his private law office, Harman opens a drawer and pulls out a gleaming, thin-bladed "butterfly" knife, which, he says, is an exact replica of the one Heath Wilkins used on Nancy Allen, a knife, he tells me, Wilkins had "sharpened to a razor edge with a black diamond file."

Finally, in his car, Harman tells me exactly where he places Heath Wilkins on his personal, two-tier hierarchy of evil among murderers. There are ordinary killers, he says, and then there are the ones so egregiously evil he could "pop a cap" on them himself.

"Pop a cap?" I ask.

"Cop talk for dropping the cyanide capsules in a gas chamber execution." (Missouri only recently shifted its mode of execution from the gas chamber to lethal injection.)

He gives me an example of another particularly brutal murderer he could execute with his own two hands: William John Wirth, a 59-year-old sex killer, now serving a life sentence.

"I could do William Wirth," he says.

But Heath Wilkins, Harman tells me, "is *scarier* than William Wirth by a long shot. Heath Wilkins is a bright, intelligent young man with a disturbed, absurd and bizarre sense of judgment. Heath is dangerous."

What clinches the case against Wilkins, exhibit A of the cold-blooded depravity of his state of mind, is, Harman says, "the trash can comparison."

The trash can comparison was the centerpiece of Harman's final successful plea to the judge for death for Wilkins. It still may turn out to be the single line that costs Wilkins his life.

It was something Wilkins said to one of his Menninger psychiatrists in describing why he decided to kill Nancy Allen instead of just taking the cash register money and leaving. Wilkins told the doctor he had nothing "personal" against Nancy Allen, except that, as a potential future witness against him, she represented an inconvenience.

"He compared her to a trash can in his path," Harman says. "If you walk around it on your way in, you have to walk around it on your way out. So the best thing to do is kick it out of your way."

"Larry's just way off," says Sean O'Brien. "I don't see how in 100 years you could just say that Heath is worse than Bill Wirth. There's a guy who raped his own granddaughter, then left a trail of rape, pillage and murder across three states. No way."

O'Brien, chief of the Kansas City public defender's office, is representing Heath Wilkins in a "post-conviction relief" action (that would allow him to withdraw his guilty plea), separate from the Supreme Court death sentence challenge. (Another of the state's public defenders, Nancy A. McKerrow, will be making the Supreme Court argument.)

O'Brien calls his client an abused, self-destructive kid who was in a psychotic state when he committed his crime, a kid who then manipulated the court into giving him the death penalty. If it's carried out, O'Brien says, it will be "a state-assisted suicide."

O'Brien points out that an independent psychiatric evaluation by the state's Department of Mental Health, which was commissioned by the Missouri Supreme Court, flatly declared Wilkins not mentally competent to waive his right to an attorney and forgo his death penalty appeal.

"That's a major defect any way you look at it, but the State Supreme Court glossed over it because they've been terribly anxious to execute somebody. They've affirmed about 70 death sentences in the last 10 years but they haven't been able to execute anyone since 1965, since they're getting reversed or stayed by the Eighth Circuit or the Supreme Court.

"They're frustrated," he says, "and along comes Heath and they thought they had a *volunteer*. They didn't care it was a 16-year-old volunteer. They just wanted to forge ahead." (In January, shortly after O'Brien spoke, Missouri carried out its first execution in 24 years.)

As for the trash can comparison, O'Brien points out Wilkins offered it at a time he was trying to manipulate the court into giving him the death penalty he knew was reserved for murderers who exhibit cold-blooded depravity.

O'Brien in no way minimizes the gravity of the crime. But he denies that the state of mind that produced it was anything like that of a cold-blooded killer. Instead, he sees it as a tragedy that wouldn't have happened if official neglect hadn't left Wilkins homeless and desperate. "Everybody along the line washed their hands of Heath," O'Brien says.

But, he adds, desperation alone was not enough to trigger the crime. In addition, there were symptoms of psychosis diagnosed by several psychiatrists — the legacy of an abused childhood typical, studies show, of juveniles who become murderers.

The evidence for that is easy to find in Wilkins's past, O'Brien says, but not the way Wilkins himself now tells it. According to Wilkins, the turning point in his life was the result of a stupid juvenile misunderstanding.

It happened when he was 12 years old, detained in a home for juveniles for petty thievery, but still with a dream of the future.

"I wanted to be in the Air Force. I loved science, I loved flying with all my heart. I hated being locked up, but I could spend all day studying flying."

Then one day that dream was shattered. "These Air Force people came in to talk about careers and I asked them if being in trouble as a juvenile would prevent me from getting into the Air Force. They said only if your crime was really serious. Now everybody had been coming down on me so much about how I had to *realize* what a serious crime it was I'd done, that I just figured — that was it. I just quit. After that I had no future. It wasn't 'till later that I learned I'd been wrong, but by then the score was against me as a law-abiding citizen."

He tells a number of similar tales of adolescent disillusionments. They don't, of course, add up to the whole story, don't explain the viciousness with which he stabbed Nancy Allen. O'Brien, in effect, calls these stories a cover-up for the history of abuse Heath no longer wishes to discuss.

Psychiatric and diagnostic records tell a different, darker story of his childhood, one that Heath will only confirm reluctantly now that he's had a reconciliation with his mother. The trouble began while he was still in the womb, when his father, a cropdusting pilot, was badly burned and scarred in a crash. The family didn't survive the aftermath, and following the divorce Heath was subjected to sexual abuse by a male baby sitter and physical abuse by a boyfriend of his mother. According to what Heath told psychiatrists and attorneys, substance abuse was forced on him at age 5, when he was fed speed by an adult relative and dropped off at kindergarten as a kind of "experiment" for the amusement of one of the adults in his house.

His only escape from the torment, he told me, was to go out into the garage and "huff gasoline" — suck the fumes into his lungs until his brain buzzed and "I'd look up at the trees and hear voices calling my name." He did that, by his recollection, at least 500 times in grade school.

There's a remarkable fantasy Wilkins expounded to a psychiatrist about a man who painted a picture and did not like the finished product. " 'This is ugly, this is helpless,' " the man in Heath's fantasy says, according to the psychiatrist's report. " 'It didn't do any good.' So he threw it away, threw it away in the trash."

It speaks to O'Brien's contention that by the time Wilkins had gotten to the point where he could compare his victim to a trash can, he had already reached a place where he himself felt used up and thrown away, like a piece of trash.

In the holding cell, I ask Wilkins directly if, in the trash can comparison, he was saying he thought his own life had become nothing but trash. Wilkins pauses for an unusually long time. "No, I'm not trying to absolve myself of responsibility," he says. "I knew it was a terrible crime. I knew I had to change my mental outlook."

Has his mental outlook changed? The question is pertinent because opponents of the death penalty, in addition to arguing that juveniles lack full moral culpability, also say juveniles ought to be spared because they have greater rehabilitative potential than adult killers. They're less hardened in crime, have more time to mature and change.

Wilkins says he dates the moment he knew he had to change his life to the night of the murder, when he came back from stabbing Nancy Allen to death and saw the look on his girlfriend's face.

He says he "felt nothing until I got back and saw her. ... It was what I saw in her face, when she'd seen I'd actually done it. See what I'm saying? ... I saw four lives destroyed, not including mine." (His girlfriend, Marjorie (Midget) Filipiak, who did not accompany Heath to Linda's Liquors, pleaded guilty to conspiracy to commit murder and received a suspended 15-year sentence and five years probation. Ray (Shades) Thompson Jr., who also stayed behind, pleaded guilty to a similar charge, and is serving 15 years in prison. Patrick Kelly (Bo) Stevens, who pleaded guilty to second-degree murder, is now in prison for life.)

It was, Wilkins says, "the worst moment of my life." He felt the enormity of what he'd done, realized he couldn't go through with other robbery-murders he'd planned and decided "to seek my own death." He says that in the first few weeks after his arrest, he tried to hang himself in his cell "night after night." It wasn't until 1986, after he'd arrived on death row, when someone put a Bible on his bed, he says, that he "got saved" and started thinking about life rather than death.

He still feels he owes a life for the one he took; in our interview, he repeatedly expresses remorse for the pain he caused the victim and her family, says he thought of writing them to tell them, but then worried he'd just hurt them more by reminding them of him. These days, he's allowed himself to think about the possibility of life enough to fantasize what he might do if he were ever free: "Go to Australia, the outback … get a pilot's license." And ride the desert thermals in lighter-than-air craft of his own design.

Needless to say, some skepticism is in order, not merely of the death row conversion but of someone who has boasted of "playing" therapy language "like Stalin played socialism."

More suggestive of change than the abstract language of contrition, perhaps, are the stories Wilkins tells about his reaction to death row life — what it's like, for instance, to watch trash-TV crime shows that are popular with other convicts.

Heath recalls watching an episode of "Unsolved Mysteries" about a cop killing. There was a re-enactment. "It showed the cop shot, dying. And this guy sitting there says 'yeah,' like 'good,' and he automatically thinks I agree with him. I can't, man, I mean he didn't have to [kill this cop]. Think of the guy's wife." Then Wilkins talks about what he says is his real fantasy: Atoning for his own crime by giving up his life to save a cop. "Maybe in a prison riot I could save a cop's life. I'm not saying it would make up for the life I took, except symbolically. I still feel I'd probably have to give up my own life, too, for that. See what I'm saying?"

Sean O'Brien calls the change Wilkins has gone through "a rehabilitative response to confinement." Perhaps it might also be called "death row therapy." Wilkins seems to have been genuinely shocked and horrified by the state's "worst killers," with whom he's now confined. Which seems somehow to have galvanized him to define himself against them.

"You know they say you are what you eat; I'm surrounded by deranged psychotic killers. That's the atmosphere I drink in. What they do is make life around them as horrible as it is inside them, you know what I'm saying? My struggle is to keep from *being* that way."

At the very least, it can't be argued against Wilkins that he's portraying himself as penitent in order to escape the executioner. The single most urgent thing he communicates to me is that he still *prefers* the executioner to lifetime confinement, the most likely alternative should the Supreme Court set aside his death sentence. Over and over again, he expresses horror at the notion of lifetime confinement. Asked how he'd react if he ended up serving life without possibility of parole, he says: "It's like somebody discussing holding their hand in a flame for an hour. It's the first few seconds I'm worried about."

I asked him if maybe people underestimated the deterrent power that the fear of lifetime confinement without parole might have.

"Absolutely," he said. "Death isn't a scary thing to someone who's hurting inside so bad they're hurting other people. They're looking for death as *a way out*."

Three and a half years after his wife's murder, I tried to reach David Allen, but his own brother doesn't know where he is. I had a brief, strained conversation with the brother, Robert Allen, who couldn't tell me what had become of David.

"He hasn't talked to me in two years."

Why?

"Blames me."

Why blame you?

"I gave her the job there," he says, barely audibly. "I was only trying to help out."

Does Robert Allen think Wilkins should live or die? He confirms that he originally favored the death penalty for Wilkins, but that when he learned that Wilkins was asking for death instead of life, Allen decided he wanted Wilkins to get life instead of death.

What about now, with Wilkins at least formally joined to a Supreme Court appeal against his death sentence?

"Whatever he *doesn't* want," Allen says. Then he pauses and says something different. "It shouldn't be *his* decision."

A TANGLED WEB FOR THE SUPREME COURT

Since 1642, when Plymouth Colony, Mass., hanged a teen-age boy for the crime of bestiality, 281 juvenile offenders have been executed in the United States. The most recent was in 1986, when Texas executed a murderer who was 17 at the time of his crime.

Although there are only 27 now facing execution for murder, juveniles commit about 9 percent of the homicides in the United States, according to Prof. Victor L. Streib of Cleveland State University's Cleveland-Marshall College of Law. Professor Streib is a recognized authority on the history of the juvenile death penalty and one of its leading opponents.

But arguing the Supreme Court cases against the juvenile death penalty has turned out to be a trickier matter than might be supposed. The American Civil Liberties Union, for instance, long a crusader against the death penalty per se, has been stymied by an internal split over the philosophical grounding for its brief against the execution of juveniles, a split which has effectively silenced it in the Wilkins case.

To understand the A.C.L.U. dilemma, it's necessary to look at the way recent Supreme Court decisions in death-penalty cases have structured the debate on the question.

If there's a continuous thread in the sometimes-contradictory outcomes of the High Court's rulings on the death penalty in the last two decades, it has been the effort to "rationalize" — some say sanitize — through multiple overlays of due process, the fact that the state is sanctioning a bloody act, a kind of retributive ritual murder. The impulse to make the ritual rational is common to the Court's 1972 decision in Furman v. Georgia, which called a temporary halt to executions, and to its 1976 decision in Gregg v. Georgia that began the process of allowing the individual states to perform executions again.

The majority in the 5-4 Furman decision to suspend capital punishment disagreed on their reasons for it. While liberals like Justice William J. Brennan Jr. condemned the death penalty as a "denial of the executed person's humanity," the line of thought that prevailed was less categorical. Not a horror of the death penalty per se, but a horror of the process in which this "unique penalty" was "so wantonly and freakishly imposed," in the words of Justice Potter Stewart. There were so many inequities and disparities in the methods used by the states to choose who should live or die, that the death penalty as imposed, Justice Stewart said, was "cruel and unusual in the same way that being struck by lightning is cruel and unusual."

This reasoning, in effect, turned out to be an invitation to those who believe in capital punishment to frame state death-penalty laws and procedures in a more "rational" way, one that exhibits "informed selectivity," as Justice Brennan called it in Furman, so that supposedly only the very worst murderers are executed. In other words: prove to the Court that a given murderer really deserves to be struck by lightning, and we'll let you electrocute him.

Central to most of the new state statutes that arose as a consequence was a separate jury consideration of the death penalty question. Often called "penalty-phase hearings," they are supposed to bring forth both aggravating and mitigating factors that the jury weighs in deciding whether the defendant is truly among the "worst" murderers.

Opponents of the juvenile death penalty have focused their arguments on what might be called presumptive mitigation of adolescence that the universally recognized turmoil of the adolescent psyche is a kind of "diminished capacity" which should exempt juveniles from the full fatal force of the death penalty statutes. If they have a presumptive incapacity to vote, drink or serve on juries, the reasoning goes, they should also be ineligible for the death penalty.

But this argument is exactly what caused the split in the liberal ranks of the A.C.L.U. Last year, a brief drafted for the A.C.L.U. in the Supreme Court appeal of William Wayne Thompson, who killed when he was 15, was then attacked by some A.C.L.U. lawyers. The challenge faulted the initial brief for its emphasis on the incapacity of juveniles to make moral, even rational decisions.

Janet Benshoff of the group's Reproductive Rights Project, complained that the A.C.L.U. was arguing in her cases that, for instance, teen-aged girls do have sufficient rational capacity to give "informed consent" to end a pregnancy without the parental notification an increasing number of states now require to discourage teen-age abortions.

After much wrangling, the two factions failed to reconcile their positions, and the A.C.L.U. failed to file briefs in either the Thompson or the Wilkins case.

Henry Schwarzschild of the A.C.L.U.'s Capital Punishment Project says the logic of Benshoff's side "forces me to say that in order to oppose restrictions on abortion, I have to favor hanging 15-year-old girls."

Benshoff calls that characterization "too weird," and warns that by taking the position that teen-agers aren't moral creatures, the A.C.L.U. might, in effect, be writing into Constitutional law an outmoded concept of juvenile autonomy that will rob adolescents of liberties they now enjoy.

Benshoff believes there is a way to transcend this controversy over metaphysics and morals and still oppose execution of juveniles. She suggests that a stronger basis for opposing the juvenile death penalty is the almost self-evident proposition that juveniles have a rehabilitative potential that hardened-in-depravity adult murderers "selected" for death by due process do not. This potential, she says — and the lifetime to develop it — should be the element of presumptive mitigation that disqualifies them for the ultimate penalty.

Oddly enough, in view of this liberal paralysis, it was the relatively conservative American Bar Association which filed the most unexpectedly eloquent brief in the Wilkins case. The Bar Association has twice voted down resolutions opposing the death penalty itself. But its Wilkins brief flatly states that it is "central to our perceptions of ourselves as a civilized society" that we don't execute offenders under the age of 18.

RON ROSENBAUM is a contributing editor of Vanity Fair and is at work on a novel for Viking.

Supreme Court, 5-4, Forbids Execution in Juvenile Crime

BY LINDA GREENHOUSE | MARCH 2, 2005

WASHINGTON, MARCH 1 — Concluding that the United States and the world have turned against the death penalty for youthful offenders, the Supreme Court ruled on Tuesday that the Constitution categorically bars capital punishment for crimes committed before the age of 18.

The 5-to-4 decision, which upheld a ruling by the Missouri Supreme Court, will move 72 people off death row in 12 states. It represented an about-face for a court that only 16 years ago rejected the argument that the execution of those who kill at the age of 16 or 17 violated the Eighth Amendment's prohibition against "cruel and unusual punishments."

Writing for the court on Tuesday, Justice Anthony M. Kennedy, who voted with the majority 16 years ago, said the new decision was necessary to keep pace with the "evolving standards of decency" that for the last 50 years have shaped the Supreme Court's view of what constitutes cruel and unusual punishments.

Justice Kennedy said that not only did 30 states — five more than 16 years ago — now reject the death penalty for juveniles, but that "it is fair to say that the United States now stands alone in a world that has turned its face against the juvenile death penalty."

Since 1990, he noted, only seven countries outside the United States have executed people for crimes they committed as juveniles, and all seven — Iran, Pakistan, Saudi Arabia, Yemen, Nigeria, China and Congo — have disavowed the practice.

There have been 19 such executions in the United States since 1990, most recently in 2003. Once the Supreme Court agreed in January of last year to decide the issue, all executions that stood to be affected by the decision were put on hold.

Justice Antonin Scalia, author of the court's last ruling on the subject, Stanford v. Kentucky, filed a dissent on the new decision in Roper

v. Simmons, No.03-633. Joined by Chief Justice William H. Rehnquist and Justice Clarence Thomas, Justice Scalia disputed nearly all of the majority's points, from how to count the various states to whether reference to the views of foreign legal systems had relevance or legitimacy.

"I do not believe that the meaning of our Eighth Amendment, any more than the meaning of other provisions of our Constitution, should be determined by the subjective views of five members of this court and like-minded foreigners," Justice Scalia said.

Justice Sandra Day O'Connor wrote a separate dissenting opinion that took issue both with the majority's assessment of the existence of a national consensus and with its view that the execution of juveniles was always disproportionate to their moral culpability. She noted that while as a legislator she would be "inclined to support" a minimum age of 18 for capital punishment, she could not find a constitutional basis for doing so as a judge.

Justice O'Connor pointedly disagreed, however, with her fellow dissenters' opposition to taking into account foreign legal developments. "This nation's evolving understanding of human dignity certainly is neither wholly isolated from, nor inherently at odds with, the values prevailing in other countries," she said.

Justice Kennedy's majority opinion was joined by Justices John Paul Stevens, David H. Souter, Ruth Bader Ginsburg and Stephen G. Breyer. Justices Stevens and Ginsburg filed a concurring opinion to say that "perhaps even more important than our specific holding today is our reaffirmation of the basic principle that informs the court's interpretation of the Eighth Amendment"; namely, that the amendment's meaning was not frozen at the time of its adoption but has evolved.

That evolution has been on lively display in recent years with respect to the death penalty. In 1988, in Thompson v. Oklahoma, the court barred the execution of those under 16 at the time of the crime. Three years ago, in Atkins v. Virginia, the court ruled that the Eighth Amendment categorically barred the execution of the mentally retarded. The contrary precedent that the Atkins decision overruled was handed down on the same day in 1989 as the ruling that the court repudiated on Tuesday, permitting the execution of those who killed at 16 or 17.

The court based the Atkins decision on its perception that a new consensus had formed in the country to reject the execution of the retarded; 16 states that had permitted such executions in 1989 had rejected them by the time the issue came back to the Supreme Court in 2000. After that decision, the attention of opponents of the death penalty immediately turned to the juvenile question, on which the development in the states since 1989 had been slower, but steady and uniformly in the direction of raising the age.

The defendant in the new case, Christopher Simmons, who was sentenced to death for a murder he committed in 1993 at 17, went back to the Missouri courts after the Atkins decision to argue that the reasoning of the retardation case should be applied to juvenile offenders.

The Missouri Supreme Court agreed, noting that five states since 1989, by legislation or judicial decision, had raised the age to 18. It ordered Mr. Simmons re-sentenced to life in prison without parole.

In their dissenting opinions on Tuesday, both Justice O'Connor and Justice Scalia were highly critical of the Missouri court, saying that it lacked authority to depart, on its own, from the Supreme Court's binding precedent. "Allowing lower courts to reinterpret the Eighth Amendment whenever they decide enough time has passed for a new snapshot leaves this court's decisions without any force," Justice Scalia said, adding, "The result will be to crown arbitrariness with chaos."

The majority did not engage in this particular debate. Instead, Justice Kennedy took the Missouri Supreme Court's opinion as a given and then proceeded through his own analysis of the factual and legal landscape.

That analysis had three parts. First was an assessment of whether American society had formed a consensus against juvenile executions. While the change was "less dramatic" than the change on the retardation question, Justice Kennedy said, it nonetheless provided the "objective indicia of consensus" that the court found to be enough in the retardation case. He noted that Congress had set a minimum age of 18 when it passed the Federal Death Penalty Act in 1994. Counting the 12 states with no death penalty, he said, a majority of the states have rejected capital punishment for juvenile crimes.

In his dissent, Justice Scalia said it made little sense to include the non-death-penalty states in this calculation, calling the majority's approach "rather like including old-order Amishmen in a consumer-preference poll on the electric car." He continued: "Of course they don't like it, but that sheds no light whatever on the point at issue." Without counting the non-death-penalty states, he said, only 18 states had legislatively rejected the execution of 16- and 17-year-olds.

The second step in the majority's analysis was to move beyond counting by states to decide, in Justice Kennedy's words, "in the exercise of our own independent judgment, whether the death penalty is a disproportionate punishment for juveniles."

He said that "three general differences between juveniles under 18 and adults demonstrate that juvenile offenders cannot with reliability be classified among the worst offenders." The differences were: "a lack of maturity and an underdeveloped sense of responsibility"; vulnerability to peer pressure; and a personality that is still in formation, making it "less supportable to conclude that even a heinous crime committed by a juvenile is evidence of irretrievably depraved character."

Justice Kennedy concluded: "When a juvenile offender commits a heinous crime, the state can exact forfeiture of some of the most basic liberties, but the state cannot extinguish his life and his potential to attain a mature understanding of his own humanity."

This analysis, too, provoked Justice Scalia's strong dissent. "By what conceivable warrant can nine lawyers presume to be the authoritative conscience of the nation?" he asked. After describing details of Mr. Simmons's crime, which involved breaking into a woman's home, binding her with tape and wire and throwing her off a bridge into a river, where she drowned, Justice Scalia said the majority had failed to justify "a constitutional imperative that prevents legislatures and juries from treating exceptional cases in an exceptional way by determining that some murders are not just the acts of happy-go-lucky teenagers, but heinous crimes deserving of death."

Justice Scalia reserved his strongest dissent for the final stage of the majority's analysis, its reference to international developments that have left the United States alone in supporting juvenile executions. In the majority opinion, Justice Kennedy said that while the court was not bound by foreign developments, "it is proper that we acknowledge the overwhelming weight of international opinion" for its "respected and significant confirmation for our own conclusions."

Justice Scalia objected that while the court had determined that "the views of our own citizens are essentially irrelevant," it had wrongly given "center stage" to the "so-called international community."

CHAPTER 6

Religious Perspectives

Though religious texts abound in verses supporting the penalty of death, religious leaders have been among the most outspoken opponents of the practice in modern times. The basis of their arguments range from recognition of God as the sole arbiter of justice to acknowledgment that the penalty often is applied in unfair and arbitrary ways. Perhaps most salient has been the Catholic Church's growing opposition to capital punishment in recent decades. In late 2018, Pope Francis issued a total rejection of the practice under all circumstances.

Reform Jews Ask Death Penalty End

BY THE NEW YORK TIMES | APRIL 26, 1959

THE HEAD OF REFORM JUDAISM in the United States called yesterday for the abolition of capital punishment.

Rabbi Maurice N. Eisendrath, president of the Union of American Hebrew Congregations, sent a message to the 858 Reform temples asking them to start a program of education and debate on the question of the death penalty.

As a guide to debate, the union's Commission on Social Action issued a pamphlet, "Man's Right to Life," written by Ruth Leigh.

The death penalty, the booklet says, "is a brutalization of the human spirit and an arrogation to vindictive men of the life-taking power which inheres only in God."

Capital punishment serves no practical purpose, Dr. Eisendrath said. It does not deter crime, he said, and it has led to the execution of innocent persons.

"Seldom are murderers with means, who can afford unlimited appeals, subjected to the death penalty," the rabbi said. "Most persons executed are poor and friendless."

Lutherans Hit Death Penalty: Aides of 3.3 Million-Member Church Favor a Ban

BY EDWARD B. FISKE | JUNE 30, 1966

KANSAS CITY, MO. JUNE 29 — The 3.3 million-member Lutheran Church in America today joined the growing list of major Protestant bodies calling for the end of capital punishment.

In doing so, however, the nation's largest Lutheran body specifically discounted obedience to the Fifth Commandment, "Thou shalt not kill," as a reason for taking this position.

Other church groups have used this argument as a justification for opposing the death penalty. A Lutheran official today termed this "sloppy thinking."

The action was taken by 688 lay and clergy delegates at the final working session of the denomination's nine-day biennial meeting here. In a resolution passed by a near-unanimous vote the Lutheran leaders called for "the abolition of capital punishment" and urged church members in places where it still exists to "encourage their legislatures to abolish it."

The statement emphasized, however, that a decision to abolish the death penalty "is not to be construed as a repudiation of the inherent power of the state to take life in the exercise of its divine mandate."

On the contrary, it continued, the state is "responsible under God" for the maintenance of justice and order and is consequently "entrusted by God with the power to take human life when the failure to do so constitutes a clear danger to the civil community."

Leaders explained that the killing of someone in self-defense by a policeman would be one example of the legitimate taking of life by a representative of the state.

In recent years a number of Protestant denominations have called for an end to the death penalty.

These include the American Baptist Convention, the Disciples of Christ, the Church of the Brethren, the Episcopal Church, the United Presbyterian Church in the U.S.A., and the Presbyterian Church in the U.S.

In some instances these groups have used the Biblical injunction against killing as a prime reason for abolishing capital punishment.

The Rev. Richard J. Niebnck, an official of the Board of Social Ministry, who was instrumental in drafting today's resolution, said, "There has been a great deal of sloppy thinking in church circles about this issue.

"The state's power to establish justice in the context of civil order ultimately means power over life and death. It is only when this power is abused — when its use does not contribute to this purpose — that killing by the state becomes wrong."

Today's resolution put the death penalty in the "abuse" category on the grounds that it "falls disproportionately upon those least able to defend themselves," makes a miscarriage of justice irrevocable, and "ends the possibility of restoring the convicted person to effective and productive citizenship."

The resolution also noted "the impossibility of demonstrating a deterrent value in capital punishment."

An official of the Board of Social Ministry said today that the agency would probably begin "right at home" in implementing last night's endorsement by the convention of the principle of guaranteed minimum income for all persons.

The Rev. Horlof M. Jensen said this morning that the agency would begin to study various proposals in this area — including the guaranteed annual income proposal of the economist Robert Theobald and the "negative income tax" idea of Milton Friedman.

"Before endorsing a specific way of achieving this goal, however," he said, "there is much that we can do in some of our own institutions where the pay scales are far below minimum."

Milestone in Death Penalty Fight, but Still a Way to Go

BY PETER STEINFELS | DEC. 22, 2007

MARIO MARAZZITI'S NAME appeared in this column on Dec. 23, 2000, almost exactly seven years ago. An Italian journalist and spokesman for the Community of Sant'Egidio, a Roman Catholic movement of lay people known for its efforts on behalf of the poor and peacemaking, he had been bustling around holiday-happy Manhattan.

He was not sightseeing or shopping for gifts, but advocating a United Nations resolution against the death penalty.

This past week, Mr. Marazziti, now 55, was back in town to finish the job. On Tuesday, the General Assembly passed a resolution calling for a moratorium on the death penalty. The resolution was nonbinding. Mr. Marazziti called it a milestone, nonetheless.

It sets "a new moral standard of justice," he said at a small gathering after the vote, making it harder for nations to ignore. It stamps the death penalty as a matter of legitimate concern for the international community, he added; it calls for the secretary general to monitor and report on the extent of executions. And, he argued, it makes it easier for countries that are "de facto abolitionist" — which he defined as ones where no one had been executed in at least a decade — to chisel their practice into law.

Tuesday's General Assembly vote was 104 nations in favor, 54 against and 29 abstaining. Among the opposed, the United States found itself lined up with Iran, Syria, Sudan, China and North Korea. All European Union nations, almost all Latin American states and United States allies like Turkey and Israel supported the resolution.

But the real vote had taken place a month earlier when the resolution was fiercely debated by the Social, Humanitarian and Cultural Committee, often simply called the Third Committee, composed of all 192 member states of the United Nations.

Opposition to the resolution had long been led by Singapore, Egypt and a few Caribbean nations like Barbados. They maintained that the death penalty was strictly an internal affair of criminal law and that the pressure to abolish it reflected a European-based form of neo-colonialism.

An anti-capital-punishment resolution introduced by Italy was defeated in 1994. In 1999, faced with similar opposition, the European Union withdrew another such resolution.

Islamic nations were also influenced by the argument that the death penalty was an intrinsic part of Islamic law and could not be renounced in principle, however flexibly it might be applied in practice.

Working with other groups opposed to the death penalty like Amnesty International, the Sant'Egidio Community set out to counter Islamic reservations by urging a moratorium rather than outright abolition, thus setting aside the question of principle. By such intermediate steps, after all, Judaism long ago and Christianity more recently had moved away from biblical affirmations of the death penalty.

To counter the accusation of European neo-colonialism, Sant'Egidio led a campaign to gather signatures from all around the world on a petition for a moratorium. Seven years ago, Mr. Marazziti delivered more than three million of those signatures to the United Nations. This November, he delivered the petition anew, now carrying five million signatures from 153 countries.

Nations opposed to the resolution still tried to block it in November with crippling amendments. Egypt mobilized the support of primarily Muslim countries, for example, with a last-minute amendment extending the resolution "to protect the lives of unborn children."

Led by the Philippines, a number of countries, including many Latin American ones that ban abortions, replied that they would sponsor a resolution on that topic but that raising it now was only a distraction from the issue at hand.

The Vatican's representative at the United Nations expressed regret that when the notion of a right to life was not applied consistently from the beginning to the end of life, the result was political maneuvering.

Egypt's amendments were defeated, and the Vatican welcomed the moratorium resolution, both in November and this week, after it was passed by the General Assembly.

On Tuesday, Mr. Marazziti repeatedly spoke of the General Assembly's action as strengthening the "culture of life," a phrase that Pope John Paul II had popularized in connection with opposition to abortion.

Asked whether he connected ending the death penalty with ending abortion, Mr. Marazziti replied that he and Sant'Egidio believed that "life should be defended from the very beginning to the end." But abolishing the death penalty, for which there were plenty of nonreligious arguments, he said, would be an important step toward a "general culture of life as a new proposal for our time."

He recognized how far the world remained from such a culture. Not only was the United Nations resolution not binding, but the support of many countries stemmed from winning over the political elite, rather than the public at large.

The Sant'Egidio Community itself won over many officials in Africa. Of the approximately 50,000 members that the movement claims, one third are African; and a major program to deal with AIDS in 10 African countries has increased Sant'Egidio's moral standing on the continent.

"We cannot promise money or use power," Mr. Marazziti said. So success rested on personal relationships and patient pleading, and he was not embarrassed by the focus on the political elites. "A leading class must sometimes take the responsibility of being a leading class," he said. But he knew that the task of changing public opinion remained.

Seven years ago, Mr. Marazziti was quick to admit that there were bigger problems in the world than the death penalty. On Tuesday, what with wars, terrorism and climate change, it was hard to argue that things had changed for the better. But what about for him personally?

His response was instantaneous. He grinned, whipped out his cellphone and clicked on the picture of his 17-month-old grandson. Culture of life, indeed!

Pope Francis Declares Death Penalty Unacceptable in All Cases

BY ELISABETTA POVOLEDO AND LAURIE GOODSTEIN | AUG. 2, 2018

ROME — Pope Francis has declared the death penalty wrong in all cases, a definitive change in church teaching that is likely to challenge Catholic politicians, judges and officials who have argued that their church was not entirely opposed to capital punishment.

Before, church doctrine accepted the death penalty if it was "the only practicable way" to defend lives, an opening that some Catholics took as license to support capital punishment in many cases.

But Francis said executions were unacceptable in all cases because they are "an attack" on human dignity, the Vatican announced on Thursday, adding that the church would work "with determination" to abolish capital punishment worldwide.

Francis made the change to the Catechism of the Roman Catholic Church, the book of doctrine that is taught to Catholic children worldwide and studied by adults in a church with 1.2 billion members. Abolishing the death penalty has long been one of his top priorities, along with saving the environment and caring for immigrants and refugees.

A majority of the world's countries — including nearly every nation in Europe and Latin America, regions that are home to large Catholic populations — have already banned the death penalty, according to Amnesty International.

The pope's decree is likely to hit hardest in the United States, where a majority of Catholics support the death penalty and the powerful "pro-life movement" has focused almost exclusively on ending abortion — not the death penalty. The pope's move could put Catholic politicians in a new and difficult position, especially Catholic governors like Greg Abbott of Texas and Pete Ricketts of Nebraska, who have presided over executions.

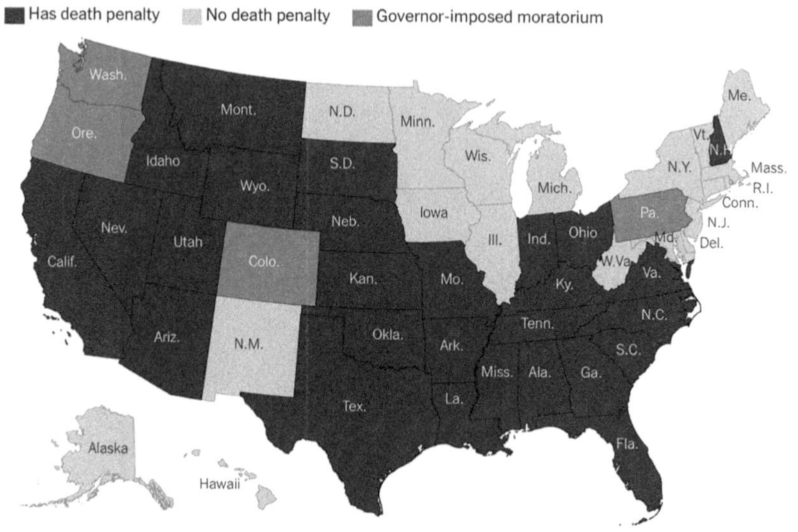

THE NEW YORK TIMES

Capital punishment is legal in 31 states. Governors have imposed moratoriums on the death penalty in four of those states.

"If you're a Catholic governor who thinks the state has the right to end human life, you need to be comfortable saying you're disregarding orthodox church teaching," said John Gehring, the Catholic program director at Faith in Public Life, a liberal-leaning advocacy group in Washington. "There isn't any loophole for you to wiggle through now."

The new ruling could also complicate the lives of American judges who are practicing Catholics.

President Trump's nominee to the Supreme Court, Judge Brett M. Kavanaugh, is Catholic, as are Chief Justice John G. Roberts Jr. and Justices Clarence Thomas, Samuel A. Alito Jr. and Sonia Sotomayor. One of the other finalists for the vacancy created by the retirement of Justice Anthony M. Kennedy was Judge Amy Coney Barrett, who is also Catholic.

In a 2002 article, Justice Antonin Scalia, who died in 2016, said, "I do not find the death penalty immoral," and added that he was confident that Catholic doctrine allowed for its use in some cases.

He wrote that it would be a bad idea if Catholic judges had to recuse themselves in death penalty cases or if Catholic governors had to promise commutations of death sentences, and commented, "Most of them would never reach the governor's mansion."

Chester L. Gillis, professor of theology at Georgetown University, described Francis's new teaching on the death penalty as "part of the regular teaching of the church" and "binding." But that does not mean that Catholics who believe differently will face penalties or be denied the sacraments.

"There are lots of other teachings in the Catholic church that not everybody abides by," he said. "Is practicing birth control a mortal sin? If true there would be a lot of couples in mortal sin."

A majority of American Catholics favor capital punishment, 53 percent, while 42 percent oppose it, according to a poll that the Pew Research Center conducted this spring. Among Americans as a whole, 54 percent are in favor and 39 percent opposed.

Cara H. Drinan, a professor of law at Catholic University of America in Washington and an expert on criminal justice reform, said Catholics should be able to accept this development because it is "perfectly consistent with Catholic teaching on a consistent ethic of life."

And yet, she said, there may be resistance.

"The land of the free has become the world's biggest jailer," Ms. Drinan said, "and even practicing Catholics have a hard time setting aside this knee-jerk reaction of 'you do the crime, you do the time.' It's part of who we are."

The new teaching builds on the teachings of Francis' two immediate predecessors. For example, in 1992, in the catechism promoted by John Paul II, who has since been canonized, the death penalty was allowed if it was "the only practicable way to defend the lives of human beings effectively against the aggressor."

"This didn't come out of nowhere," said John Thavis, a Vatican expert and author. "John Paul II and Benedict laid the ground work; he's taking the next logical step."

"I think this will be a big deal for the future of the death penalty in the world," he added. "People who work with prisoners on death row will be thrilled, and I think this will become a banner social justice issue for the church."

Sergio D'Elia, the secretary of Hands Off Cain, an association that works to abolish capital punishment worldwide, said, "Now even the most far-flung parish priest will teach this to young children."

Mario Marazziti, the coordinator of the global anti-death penalty campaign of the Community of Sant'Egidio, a Catholic organization in Rome, said Francis had shifted the church's teachings from "the practical opposition" of the old catechism, which acknowledged the church's historical acceptance of the death penalty, to "absolute rejection," which "becomes a normal part of teaching and commitment on the part of the faithful."

"It becomes binding for bishops, defense of life from the initial state through all its phases to the very end, even for those who are guilty," he said.

"If you don't accept this, you are disobedient, as you would be if you didn't accept other teachings," he said. "There is no margin for disagreement."

It could set off a backlash among American Catholic traditionalists who have already cast Francis as dangerously inclined to change or compromise church teaching on other issues, like permitting communion for Catholics who have divorced and remarried without getting a church annulment.

The majority of the world's executions take place in five countries: China, Iran, Saudi Arabia, Iraq and Pakistan. The United States was No. 8 on the list in 2017, according to Amnesty International.

Recently, there have been calls in some countries to restore the death penalty. In the Philippines, a primarily Catholic country, for example, President Rodrigo Duterte has been pushing to reimpose it.

In Africa, capital punishment exists in several countries, but a 2009 synod of African bishops called for a "total and universal abolition of the death penalty."

In 2015, four Catholic media outlets in the United States published a joint editorial calling for the death penalty to be abolished. They included the liberal-leaning National Catholic Reporter and the conservative-leaning National Catholic Register.

But many conservative Catholics took exception. The Rev. C. John McCloskey III, an influential teacher and confidant of countless American politicians and civic leaders, has written that the church's doctrine "does not and never has advocated unqualified abolition of the death penalty."

Francis spoke about his opposition to the death penalty when he visited the United States in 2015, saying in his address to the United States Congress that "every life is sacred, every human person is endowed with an inalienable dignity, and society can only benefit from the rehabilitation of those convicted of crimes."

On that trip, he visited a Pennsylvania prison and met with a few inmates and their families. He also wrote a detailed letter that year to the International Commission against the Death Penalty, arguing that capital punishment "does not render justice to the victims, but rather fosters vengeance."

In it, he made two arguments that specifically spoke to the American context: The death penalty is illegitimate because many convictions have later been found to be in error and have been overturned, and because executions of prisoners in some states have been badly botched.

Sister Helen Prejean, whose advocacy for prisoners on death row was portrayed in the film "Dead Man Walking," said that Francis had once written a letter that helped spare a man on death row in Oklahoma, and that she was certain he was well aware of the death penalty debate in the United States.

She said the only time she met Francis — attending Mass with him in the small chapel in his guesthouse in January 2016 — he asked what had happened to a prisoner in Texas whom she had enlisted his help in trying to save from execution. She told him the man had been put to death the night before.

On Thursday, she said: "It's a happy day. I'm clicking my heels. What I'm particularly delighted about is there's no loopholes. It's unconditional."

But she added: "This is just a change in the doctrine, and it's on paper. We've still got to move it into the pews and make it active."

ELISABETTA POVOLEDO reported from Rome, and **LAURIE GOODSTEIN** from New York. **ADAM LIPTAK** contributed reporting from Washington, and **SEWELL CHAN** from New York.

CHAPTER 7

Medical Perspectives

When it comes to the death penalty, medical professionals face a unique dilemma. Ethically, doctors are committed to saving lives, and the American Medical Association's guidelines prohibit doctors from participating in an execution. However, without a physician's guidance, lethal injections are often botched by prison staff, resulting in unnecessary pain for the condemned prisoner. These articles present perspectives on the role of physicians in the execution process as well as doctors' views on capital punishment.

The Kemmler Execution: Dr. C. E. Spitzka Tells Doctors and Lawyers All About It

BY THE NEW YORK TIMES | NOV. 11, 1890

AN ADDRESS AND DEBATE on the execution of William Kemmler by electricity occupied the attention of the Society of Medical Jurisprudence in its new meeting room at 17 West Forty-third Street, last night. Dr. C. E. Spitzka delivered the address and described in detail the scene of the execution. He said that he was not an advocate of execution by electricity, but he regarded the evils of that method as much less than the evils of hanging. The guillotine was his preference as a means of inflicting capital punishment.

Dr. Spitzka said that he had witnessed a number of executions, and usually there was no difficulty in picking out the person that was to suffer. On the occasion of the Kemmler execution, however, when the

Warden, the prisoner, the clergyman, and assistant keepers entered the room where the fatal chair stood he could not tell which one was to suffer the penalty. There was nothing in Kemmler's appearance or demeanor to indicate that he was the ill-fated man. In all of the many steps preliminary to the turning on of the electric current the Warden was aided greatly by the coolness and pluck of the prisoner. The doctor thought that many of the preliminary steps taken in Kemmler's case were unnecessary and should be omitted when the new law was again enforced.

The voltometer did not work at the time of the execution and Dr. Spitzka's belief was that it was not expected to work. There was no way, therefore, by which the medical witnesses were able to tell the volting of the current. Nobody was permitted to enter the dynamo room. The doctor thought that the current used on Kemmler was about 700 volts.

"In my opinion as a medical man," said Dr. Spitzka, "Kemmler was dead within an infinitesimal part of a second after the current was turned on." Convulsions followed the introduction of the electric current into the man's body. Dr. Spitzka pronounced the man dead after the current had been turned on about seventeen seconds, and he was perfectly willing to shoulder the responsibility for so doing. The pulse was absent and the pupil of the eye gave no sign of life. The doctor said that he was now satisfied that he made a mistake in ordering the current turned on a second time. But the muscular convulsions and emissions of air by the dead man threw the spectators into a state bordering on a panic. Demoralization almost prevailed in the room. One man had to be assisted out and one of the doctors was obliged to thrust his head out of a window to get a breath of fresh air. Blood dripped from one of Kemmler's fingers and many persons in the room observing that fact, exclaimed: "He can't be dead, for there is blood dripping." So intense was the muscular convulsion that one of Kemmler's thumbs had been driven into the finger. The fact that blood dripped from the wound, the doctor said, was by no means a sign of lingering life. Blood might dribble from a human body three or four days after death.

One of the phenomena observed by Dr. Spitzka was that after the fatal current had passed into Kemmler's body whenever he pressed a finger against the dead man's flesh there would appear distinct marks, which would subsequently become self-obliterated. This is one of the reputed signs of life. After the body was thoroughly dissected, the heart and lungs taken out, and the brains were laid at least eighteen feet away from the body, this same phenomenon was observable. Dr. Spitzka says that he pressed the flesh of the dead man with his finger fifty times and the result was the same in each case.

Dr. Spitzka favored the amendment of the electrical execution law so that it will provide for the construction of just one plant in this State where all executions shall occur under the direction of a competent electrician. The engine and dynamos should be constructed especially for the purpose and the dynamos should be capable of generating a current of at least 3,000 volts. Instead of applying the electrodes to the spine, the doctor thought it would be as well and in some respects better to make the victim's neck the point of contact. A collar could be so constructed as to hold even the most violent criminal firmly. The method used in Kemmler's case was unnecessarily trying to the nerves of the prisoner and it involved the cutting away of portions of the prisoner's clothing to get at the base of the spine. Should it ever happen that the person to be executed was a woman, this operation would be attended with much difficulty and embarrassment.

"The execution of Kemmler was a more decent and dignified execution of the law than any other I have ever seen," said Dr. Spitzka. "That the admission to the chamber of death of persons who had never before seen an execution and know nothing whatever of the effect of electricity on the human body, led to many extravagant and erroneous statements I really believe. There was no warrant in law for the presence of such persons."

Dr. Carlos McDonald agreed with Dr. Spitzka in his general conclusions. He remarked that the physicians who were summoned to the execution as witnesses were not consulted about any of the arrangements, and they were not permitted to see the source of the death-dealing current. He accidentally went into the dynamo room and was promptly shoved out by somebody in there. This was during the interval between the first and second applications of the current to Kemmler. While in the secret room he observed a bunch of electric lamps burning dimly. Both Dr. Spitzka and Dr. McDonald agreed that if the first current had been continued from three to five seconds longer Kemmler would not have made a move.

Remarks were also made by Dr. Sayre, Dr. Brill, and Dr. Landor Carter Gray, President of the society.

The annual election of the society will occur at the next monthly meeting. Officers wore nominated last night, the Hon. David McAdam heading the list as the only nominee for President.

The Penalty of Death

BY DR. AUSTIN FLINT | AUG. 7, 1898

IT IS LIKELY TO BE a difficult task to convince the people, or even the few who think and reason for the people, that criminology is a most useful science; and that the utility of the methods which have brought this science to its present state must be so impressed upon lawmakers and jurists as to produce radical changes in the existing systems of criminal jurisprudence. The alternative is a continued increase in crime, with its attendant pecuniary burdens, and increased danger to our social organization. Certain statistical facts bearing upon this question must be accepted. The annual cost of the machinery for the detection and punishment of crime in the United States, according to a recent report of the Ohio Board of State Charities, is $59,000,000. The half-century closing with 1899 will probably show an increase of more than fivefold in the proportion of those imprisoned for crime. In 1850 the ratio of prisoners to population was 1 to 3,442. In 1890 it was 1 to 757. The expense borne by the people is not limited to the punishment and support of criminals, but is immensely extended by individual losses in crimes against property. Restitution to the loser has a very small place in the treatment of crime. The controlling idea is punishment of the criminal, and justice to the victim is but little considered. What wonder is it, then, that crimes against property are compounded by the injured at the price of partial restitution! If the ratio of increase of crime should continue, a revolution in criminal jurisprudence within the next half century is inevitable.

Advanced criminologists are almost a unit in accepting the idea of intelligent treatment instead of punishment of criminals; but while they eliminate punishment, it is an error to suppose that the treatment of criminals relieves them of the consequences of criminal acts. Criminologists advocate measures for the prevention of crime, the reform of the criminal and his restoration to usefulness when possible, and, above all, the protection of society against incurable criminals. Intelligent treatment can be based only on a knowledge of the natural history of criminals and what may properly be called their morbid anatomy and the pathology of crime. It is at once evident that I am looking at crime from the point of view of a physician; and, indeed, the methods that have been used most successfully in the investigation of disease may well be applied to the study of crime, which is the most important and dangerous disease affecting the social system. Whatever may be the cause of disease, and however much physical and mental ailments may be due to the ignorance, faults, vices, or even crimes of those afflicted, it is the province of the physician to alleviate sufferings, restore health, and save life, however worthless or even dangerous to society some lives may be. The element of punishment does not enter into our treatment of patients; we do not kill even to relieve hopeless suffering or to spare society the pain of caring for the incurable insane, idiotic, imbecile, or deformed; much less do we induce disease in order to learn to cure it or to deter others from vices which surely lead to physical and mental maladies. We study disease on scientific principles; and we endeavor to become acquainted with it in all its phases, regarding it as an enemy to human happiness which it is our duty to combat by every means that can be used for its prevention, cure, or the mitigation of its ravages.

We recognize that disease is always with us. When all shall be born without taint or defect or danger of inheritance from the misfortunes or sins of their ancestors, shall have most judicious care until able to care for themselves, shall learn how to live in exact accordance with natural laws, and shall be free from inordinate appetites, ambitions and passions, there may be no disease and the race may then be subject only to accidents or the inevitable decay of old age. When to all this are added freedom from envy, hatred, and malice, general content and success in the pursuit of happiness, with universal recognition of natural social laws, there may be no crime, but now crime must be recognized as the greatest of social problems. As physicians study disease without prejudice or passion, so crime should be studied, as the final object in the study of disease is to subject it to intelligent treatment, so the object in the study of crime should be to treat it in the best interest of society. It is all very well to talk of human justice, but who shall fix the standard? And is it not true that so-called justice now includes the idea of vengeance, punishment, retaliation? When criminology shall have advanced so far that our lawmakers and those who administer justice become educated to a recognition of its scientific principles, punishment of crime will be replaced by judicious treatment of the criminal; without sentimentality, the treatment of criminals will be tinged with humanity, but in the words of an eminent authority, "It is not enough that criminal jurisprudence should be humane; it must also be intelligent."

Much study has of late years been given to what may be termed the anatomical characters of crime, as shown by stigmata and signs of physical degeneration, but many individuals with distinct signs of degeneration are not criminals in the sense that they ever are guilty of crime, and many criminals present no evidence of physical degeneration. Future study may enable the criminologist to recognize positive physical evidence of criminality, but at present a careful study of the moral characters of criminals seems likely to produce the best results.

In the diagnosis of crime the dispassionate and rigid application of scientific principles is most important. Judges, controlled largely by precedent and ancient jurisprudence and unaccustomed to scientific methods, and juries usually selected for want of intelligence and interest in current affairs, influenced by sympathy or the spirit of revenge, and often swayed by eloquence instead of cold reason, are expected to settle most delicate points in criminal diagnosis and responsibility for criminal acts. Under existing methods, scientific experts, far from giving aid, add confusion to criminal jurisprudence by conflicting testimony, and who shall decide which expert advocate is right? The true value of expert testimony can be estimated only by a disinterested expert. It must be remembered that truth is immutable, and with sufficient positive data, it's impossible that two contradictory scientific opinions should have equal value. Until judges can obtain and will make use of competent and disinterested scientific advice there will continue to be many miscarriages of so-called justice. How such advice is to be secured is a problem to be solved by intelligent legislative bodies. The prospect for even a recognition of this as a question for consideration at the hands of our lawmakers is not encouraging.

The prognosis of criminality, taking into account the usual treatment of the criminal, is not very difficult or uncertain. If the crime itself has certain fixed limits of punishment, and that is all, it is easy to predict the future of one convicted of his first offense. He is practically marked for life as an outcast and an enemy of society; he is thrown in with criminals by profession, and the spirit of revenge and antagonism to law is fostered; an honest life is rendered so difficult as to be practically impossible; he is one more added to the criminal classes. This system is so patent and so terrible and inimical to the best interests of society that it is well recognized. A most important step toward correction of this evil is the indeterminate sentence and the reformatory system, and, better still, these combined with the probation system of Massachusetts. A full discussion of the systems would be out of place; but it may be said here that their results are simply astounding. In a recent investigation of the Elmira Reformatory, it appeared that 81.9 per cent of the men paroled prior to September, 1893, were reformed according to the estimate of the managers. Taking, however, a total of 1,772 prisoners paroled prior to Sept. 30, 1887, definite information was obtained in regard to 1,125; and it was ascertained that 78.5 per cent had not fallen into crime, or 51.28 per cent of the total of 1,772 paroled. It is said that the results of the probation system, with supervision and no imprisonment, are even more striking in reducing the extent of crime.

It is not difficult to recognize the habitual criminal and the confirmed and permanent enemy of our social system. Society must be protected against him as against wild beasts or pestilence. A simple method of such protection, and one which was long employed, even in countries of the highest civilization, was by killing, attended with various penalties more or less cruel and revolting, intended to deter others from committing crime. While this certainly removed social enemies, it gradually appeared that it did not deter; and the pain of death, which is now practically confined to the crime of murder, is all that remains. Whether the punishment of death for murder actually deters is by some considered an open question; certainly public executions do not. The death penalty is seldom swift and is always uncertain. For the years 1882 to 1891, inclusive, the number of murders in the United States increased from 1,467 to 5,906. In 1882 8 per cent of the murders were executed and in 1891 only 2 per cent. Popular dissatisfaction with the uncertainty of punishment for murder was expressed by the facts that in ten years the legal executions numbered 1,246 and the lynchings 1,576. These statistics were collected by Gen. Newton Martin Curtis of New York, a vigorous opponent of the death penalty.

As important as are measures for the prevention of disease, such as public and private sanitation, quarantine, and vaccination, are those for the prevention of crime. Moral sanitation, by improvement in the surroundings of the poor, drainage from our large cities of the refuse youthful population into the rural districts, amelioration of the condition of the young who labor under oppressive taskmasters, and, best of all, suitable education, constitute one way of preventing vice and crime. A great fault in our social system is unsuitable education, unfitting many who should labor with their hands for occupations proper to their station in life and crowding the already overflowing class of educated poor. Our public schools, admirable as they may seem, much more frequently fail than succeed in preparing the children of the masses for their life's work. Certain studies, even if successfully pursued, give worse than useless accomplishments when they take the place of proper manual training. The Elmira Reformatory is really the best school that I know of for the social class which it educates. Its only drawback is the stigma of crime which attaches to its graduated. The entire school system of great cities is, in my opinion, in pressing need of information; a great part of the education there acquired tends to swell the number of unemployed and has little value as a means of honest livelihood.

Of all the preventives of crime, respect for law is, perhaps, the most efficient. In our free country the object of law should be to protect personal rights and personal liberty, and to secure the greatest happiness to the greatest number; and to this end laws should be intelligent, free from prejudice and bigotry, and they should never oppress one class for the benefit of another. One great evil is the constant creation of artificial crimes by statute. Every intelligent man or woman knows that certain offenses against the person or against property are crimes, and that certain ordinances are necessary for the preservation of public order, health, and comfort; but all have a sense of personal liberty and personal rights, which organized society cannot properly invade. It is difficult to convince the people that an act which is harmless and lawful at one time is criminal an hour later; that a citizen may rightly be arrested for buying or selling milk or bread at a time when he may lawfully buy tobacco or sweetmeats; that he may be induced under various pretexts, by an officer of the law, to commit an offense that offends no one, so that he may receive exemplary punishment. All these conditions exist in the City of New York, and they certainly do not promote respect for law, even in the law-abiding and orderly classes.

An ideal measure of prevention of crime is the rendering of crime unprofitable; and with many our social system has rendered it a necessity. Dugdale, the author of that remarkable study of crime called "The Jukes," says: "We must dispossess ourselves of the idea that crime does not pay," and again, "Those who do minor crimes commit about 100 to 150 offenses to one commitment, while those who go for 'big money' get caught once out of five times." The sufferer from a crime against property finds it more to his advantage to treat with the offender than to bring him to justice; and in many instances he is himself deprived of his liberty in a house of detention while the criminal is at large on bail. How crime may be made unprofitable and honesty always the best policy, how restitution, instead of additional inconvenience and injury, may be made to the innocent sufferer, are problems as difficult as they are important.

At some future time, probably very remote, there will be no such thing as human punishment, and all criminals will be subjected to scientific treatment. The indeterminate sentence and a probation system will eventually become universal. This era will bring about more extended prevention, a large proportion of cures, and better protection of society. As criminology advances, we shall be able to separate the curable from the incurable criminal, reclaiming one and protecting society against the other. If the idea of vengeance be eliminated, we shall be able to treat intelligently the criminal by passion and the criminal by occasion, who really are not criminals, as physicians treat an acute and self-limited disease. Crime will then be regarded as a moral disease, and the criminal as a patient. It is not to be understood that, the idea of punishment being eliminated, the chronic criminal will not be made to suffer and not be restrained. There should be no difference practically between the treatment of a confirmed criminal and a dangerous lunatic; the one as well as the other should be prevented from doing injury. This idea is not Utopian. It will be realized, probably in the distant future, by a dispassionate study of criminology and penology, when these sciences are pursued in the same unemotional and unsentimental manner as we study the science of medicine, but there are great obstacles in the way of progress in this direction. The greatest of these is capital punishment, the very embodiment of the idea of retribution and vengeance. This must disappear. It is more than 3,000 years since it was written, "Who so sheddeth man's blood, by man shall his blood be shed," and "Eye for eye, tooth for tooth, hand for hand, foot for foot." Revenge does no good; it is a feeling born of passion which has no place in either criminal or civil jurisprudence. It is sometimes justified, but without justice, by public sentiment, as in homicides in retaliation for crimes against the family, or in lynchings for atrocious murders; but in these instances the wreaking of private or popular vengeance is an expression of want of confidence in law. Both society and law justify the taking of life in self-defense, or on occasions of great danger to preserve discipline; but this is quite different from the deliberate taking of life in cold blood after a formal trial. We certainly should be able to prevent a murderer from repeating his crime without committing a legalized murder, and the only logical support that remains for capital punishment is that it may be deterrent. There are, however, some apparently strong arguments supported by statistics in favor of capital punishment. It has been said that murders always increase in frequency in proportion as the severity of punishment for this crime is relaxed, and statistics from Belgium, Italy, Great Britain, Switzerland, and France are cited in support of this view; but in order to deter, the death penalty must be prompt and certain, and this cannot obtain under our present penal system. On the other hand, it is generally admitted that public executions are demoralizing and do not deter. The history of murderers almost always shows a degree of moral insensibility, which is perhaps comprehended only by the criminal classes. In many instances, executed criminals display a vanity and bravado which lead them to pose as heroes, and they are so regarded by their class. Others are brought into a sort of hysterical condition, and make emotional displays of repentance and "change of heart." Emotional repentance of this kind is a delusion and a snare; it has no element of true repentance or of remorse. If there is any one thing that has been definitely ascertained by criminologists, it is that the born or habitual criminal has no remorse, even when he has committed murder. Bruce Thompson has made a careful study of this interesting question. He examined 400 criminals convicted of murder with premeditation and sentenced to death. Only three of this number expressed remorse, and it is doubtful if, in these instances, it was genuine. It is now considered certain that when there is no real remorse or repentance, we have to do with an incurable criminal who cannot be deterred from committing crime by the exemplary punishment of others. In my opinion, the death penalty does not deter, and if this be admitted, the last vestige of justification of capital punishment is swept away. Nevertheless, under our laws, those convicted of capital crimes must be sentenced to death. Judges, whatever may be their opinions, have no alternative; law-abiding citizens on juries must do their duty; if experts be permitted to aid in acquitting the guilty on the plea of irresponsibility, other experts should not hesitate to aid in carrying out the law; but the death penalty, so long as it remains in our system of criminal law, should be sure and prompt. The strict and impartial enforcement of a law affords the best means of determining whether or not it fulfills its objects.

A true physician is the embodiment of mercy and philanthropy. His mission is to relieve suffering, restore health, and save life. He should represent the best sentiments of society, and he cannot consistently countenance the taking of human life. When it is necessary, even, to destroy an unborn child to save the life of the mother, it is done with extreme reluctance and repugnance for the act. Until physicians feel justified in killing sufferers from incurable diseases, the hopelessly insane, the deformed and idiotic — which will never occur — they will not be justified in countenancing in any way the death penalty, which is simply legalized murder. Savages kill those who become burdens to them, but not civilized peoples, illuminated by the light of medical science. We are fully justified in protecting ourselves from the dangerous and incurable insane by perpetual confinement, and we are equally justified in treating in the same way the habitual criminal, who is more dangerous than the insane, as he has intelligence, acting with method and in concert with others; but these measures of protection should be tempered with mercy. Society was none the less protected when Pinel, in 1792, struck the chains from the unfortunate lunatics in the Bicêtre, whose conditions of restraint were horrible beyond description, or after Howard inaugurated prison reforms in 1793. We must look to the physician and the criminologist for real reforms in the future, and it is not without its use to compare the criminal with the patient and the treatment of crime with the treatment of disease.

Focus on Doctors and Executions

BY LAWRENCE K. ALTMAN | MARCH 20, 1994

CONTROVERSY OVER THE participation of doctors in executions has led four leading medical and human rights groups to recommend changes in state and Federal laws to insure that they do not require physicians to violate professional ethics.

After reviewing each state's laws and regulations on executions, the groups reported that executions often required doctors to violate professional ethics.

Of the 36 states that have the death penalty, 28 require the presence of a doctor at the execution, according to the report. Twenty-three states require that a physician pronounce or determine death in executions, a violation of the widely respected ethical opinions of the American Medical Association.

The study was conducted by the American College of Physicians in Philadelphia, the Physicians for Human Rights in Boston, the Human Rights Watch in New York and the National Coalition to Abolish the Death Penalty in Washington.

The groups did not take a position on the death penalty itself.

STANDARDS IN CONFLICT

Federal rules adopted by the Justice Department in 1992 proposed using lethal injections for execution and required that at least one doctor attend the execution and pronounce death.

But the American Medical Association's ethical guidelines prohibit doctors from assisting in, witnessing or attending executions. The guidelines also ban doctors from rendering technical advice to workers carrying out an execution, and from monitoring, on site or at a distance, the heartbeat or other vital signs of the condemned during the execution process.

Yesterday's report urged the medical boards that issue and revoke medical licenses in each state to define doctors' participation in executions as unethical conduct and to take appropriate disciplinary action against violators. No state is known to have done so.

The A.M.A. guidelines also prohibit doctors from prescribing or administering tranquilizers and other psychotropic drugs that are part of the execution procedure. But doctors may ethically provide tranquilizers at the specific voluntary request of a condemned person to help relieve pain or anxiety in anticipation of an execution.

The A.M.A. clearly distinguished between pronouncing and certifying death in an execution. To the A.M.A., pronouncing a death requires the doctor to monitor the condemned person during execution and determine the exact moment of death; certifying, which does not require the doctor to be present at the execution or to monitor the death, is considered ethical.

'A FAIRLY FINE LINE'

"It is a fairly fine line," said Dr. H. Jack Geiger, the president of the Physicians for Human Rights, "but the central intent is that if you are a doctor, you are not part of this process."

Kirk Johnson, the A.M.A.'s general counsel, said in an interview that his organization would refer any violation it learned about to a state licensing board.

The new report said that the A.M.A.'s guidelines should become part of all state laws and regulations on the death penalty, and laws that mandate physician presence or pronouncement of death should be changed to specifically exclude participation.

"Execution is not a medical procedure, and is not within the scope of medical practice," the report concluded. It also stated that "physicians are clearly out of place in the execution chamber, and their participation subverts the core of their professional ethics" including violation of the cardinal rule of doing no harm.

Since the Supreme Court allowed reinstatement of the death penalty in 1976, many states have allowed executions by injection of drugs.

Doctors have been called on to prescribe the lethal drug, insert the needle and tubing to deliver it, and to inspect, test and maintain lethal injection devices, the report said.

BROADER RIFT IS SEEN

Although no state that uses lethal injections actually requires a doctor to be the executioner, only New Jersey specifically excludes physicians from that role.

The clash over physician participation in executions involves a broader conflict: the authority of a state versus the ethical responsibilities of a profession.

Doctors have a duty to obey laws, Mr. Johnson, the A.M.A. official, said, "but there is no medical or public policy need to have a physician actively involved in either the planning or the execution itself, and on that basis, we think we can maintain a strong stance."

Dr. Geiger, the president of Physicians for Human Rights and a professor of community medicine at the City University of New York Medical School, said states never had trouble executing criminals by any method.

"It adds nothing to the process to hang a white cloak around the execution," Dr. Geiger said in an interview. "The implication that medical participation is essential to implement an execution is wrong and very often comes across as an attempt to put a human face on what cannot be called a humane process, whether one agrees or not with the death penalty."

In Illinois in 1990, many medical organizations lost appeals to then-Gov. James Thompson urging that the state not use doctors to implement the execution of Charles Walker. Three doctors did assist in his execution, and a few months later, the Illinois Legislature passed a bill providing for the anonymity of all people participating in executions in the state.

Doctors See Way to Cut Suffering in Executions

BY DENISE GRADY | JUNE 23, 2006

A FLOOD OF LAWSUITS challenging lethal injection as cruel and unusual has stalled executions in some states and may prompt others to abandon them. And a Supreme Court ruling last week made it easier for death-row prisoners to file such suits.

But medical experts say the current method of lethal injection could easily be changed to make suffering less likely. Even the doctor who devised the technique 30 years ago says that if he had it to do over again, he would recommend a different method.

Switching to an injection method with less potential to cause pain could undercut many of the lawsuits. But so far, in this chapter of the nation's long and tangled history with the death penalty, no state has moved to alter its lethal injection protocol.

At the core of the issue is a debate about which matters more, the comfort of prisoners or that of the people who watch them die. A major obstacle to change is that alternative methods of lethal injection, though they might be easier on inmates, would almost certainly be harder on witnesses and executioners.

With a different approach, death would take longer and might involve jerking movements that the prisoner would not feel but that would be unpleasant for others to watch.

"Policy makers have historically considered the needs of witnesses in devising protocols" for execution, said Dr. Mark Dershwitz, a professor of anesthesiology at the University of Massachusetts who has testified about the drugs used in lethal injection.

"There's an innumerably long list of medications that can be given to cause someone to die," Dr. Dershwitz said. But, he added, the emphasis on ensuring a speedy death may have prevented states from considering all the options.

Deborah W. Denno, a Fordham University law professor who is an expert on execution methods, said speculation about whether any states would change their procedures was "the question of the moment." Professor Denno said some states might tinker with their procedures just enough to avoid court cases.

And Dr. Jay Chapman, a forensic pathologist who created the nation's first lethal injection protocol, in Oklahoma in 1977, said that were he to do it once more, he would not recommend the three-drug concoction now in widespread use.

Instead, Dr. Chapman said, an overdose of one drug, a barbiturate — the method veterinarians use to end the lives of sick animals — would painlessly cause prisoners to lose consciousness, stop breathing and die. "Hindsight is always 20/20," he said.

Even some opponents of the death penalty favor such a change in lethal injection technique, reasoning that if execution cannot be banned, it should at least be made more humane.

Dr. Chapman's original approach, still the policy in the federal prison system and in most of the 37 death-penalty states that use lethal injection, calls for an overdose of a barbiturate, sodium thiopental, which causes unconsciousness and in sufficient doses can also halt breathing. The sodium thiopental is followed by two other drugs: pancuronium bromide, or Pavulon, which causes paralysis and halts breathing as well, and potassium chloride, which stops the heart within seconds.

But opponents of lethal injection say that in some cases, the second and third drugs may cause severe suffering. They argue that the drugs may be mishandled because most doctors and nurses refuse to participate in executions, leaving the responsibility to people with less training.

If the sodium thiopental did not work because the dose was too low, for example, or if the drugs were given in the wrong order, an inmate could still be conscious when the paralyzing drug and the potassium were injected. In that case, the paralyzing agent would cause a feeling of suffocation. And the potassium chloride would cause a burning sensation, muscle cramping and chest pain like that of a heart attack.

The pain from the potassium would not last long: once the drug stopped the heart, the person would lose consciousness in 10 to 15 seconds, Dr. Dershwitz said. But while the pain lasted, the inmate would be paralyzed and unable to complain, and would appear serene to witnesses.

Pavulon "gives a false sense of peacefulness," said Dr. David A. Lubarsky, chairman of anesthesiology at the University of Miami.

Indeed, because drugs like Pavulon can mask suffering, many states outlaw them for animal euthanasia.

Execution by barbiturate alone would take longer than the current method, Dr. Dershwitz said. Although prisoners would quickly lose consciousness and stop breathing, they could not be pronounced dead until electrical activity in the heart had stopped. That could take as long as 45 minutes.

In addition, Dr. Dershwitz said, barbiturates could cause "significant involuntary jerking" that would be disturbing to witnesses even though an unconscious prisoner would not feel it.

Intravenous barbiturates are not the only option, Dr. Dershwitz said. Drugs could also be injected into a muscle instead of a vein, to avoid another source of lawsuits: pain among inmates whose veins are hard to find. But injection into a muscle would take much longer to work than the intravenous method.

Another possibility might be an oral dose of barbiturates, like those doctors in Oregon can prescribe to assist suicide of some terminally patients. But prisoners would have to swallow the pills, and Professor Denno said there had never been a procedure in which prisoners had been required to participate in their own executions, essentially agreeing to commit suicide.

Dr. Chapman said that when he first proposed the three-drug technique, he imagined that it would be carried out by people with enough medical training to start intravenous lines, mix and measure the drugs, and give them in the right order.

He was then Oklahoma's chief medical examiner, and came up with the formula at the request of a legislator who was looking for a humane alternative to the electric chair. His idea became law in Oklahoma and was also adopted by 36 other states.

Once the lethal injection laws were passed, professional groups like the American Medical Association, state medical societies and associations for anesthesiologists and nurses quickly distanced themselves, saying it would be unethical for members to participate. That creates a Catch-22 in which the medical establishment refuses to perform lethal injections and yet says no one else is qualified to do so.

Although some doctors and nurses do help in executions, lethal injection in many states is carried out by paramedics, technicians or other prison employees who do not have special training in anesthesia.

Dr. Chapman said that his original protocol had called for enough barbiturate to cause death by itself and that he had added the Pavulon just as a backup, and the potassium chloride to speed the process by stopping the heart quickly. "I think the whole concept of execution is that it's carried out rapidly," he said.

Whether inmates have actually felt pain or suffocation from lethal injection is not known with certainty.

"I don't think any human has had a giant bolus of potassium chloride injected and then come back to chat about it," Dr. Lubarsky said.

But in February a federal judge in California said execution records showed that some prisoners might have suffered. He gave the state two options: either a doctor had to be present to make sure a condemned inmate was unconscious before the second and third drugs were injected, or the execution had to be performed with sodium thiopental alone.

California found two anesthesiologists who agreed to attend its next scheduled execution, of Michael Morales, a murderer. But both doctors later withdrew, and the state said it could not find other medical experts to help carry out the sentence. The execution has been postponed at least until September, when the court will examine the state's lethal injection protocol.

In challenging the protocol, Mr. Morales's lawyer, the onetime Whitewater prosecutor Kenneth W. Starr, cited an article published last year in The Lancet, a British medical journal. The main author was Dr. Lubarsky.

The researchers obtained toxicology reports on blood taken after death from 49 executed prisoners in four states, and found that 43 percent had levels of sodium thiopental so low that they might have suffered during execution.

"The data suggest that some people are awake," Dr. Lubarsky said.

But other anesthesiology experts, even some who oppose the death penalty, have challenged the findings, saying many of the blood samples were taken too long after death to give a reliable measure of what the drug's level was during execution.

Dr. Lubarsky acknowledged that the findings were being disputed and said he and his colleagues were doing additional research.

"We may find that we're wrong," he said. "We'll continue to search for a better understanding of what's going on, one that will hopefully help inform and guide the discussion taking place around this issue."

Compassionate Capital Punishment

BY CHUCK KLOSTERMAN | AUG. 8, 2014

A physician friend oversees the lethal-injection program in another state. I say this is unethical. He says just the opposite. Before him, he says, executions were often prolonged and painful. Now they are fast and painless. Because the state will continue the program with or without him, he feels that his work is humanitarian in nature. Who's right?

NAME WITHHELD, NEW YORK

TO ANSWER THIS QUESTION, I need to operate from the premise that capital punishment is fundamentally unethical. I'm not doing so to forward any kind of political position; in this case, my personal views on capital punishment are irrelevant. The nature of your question, however, requires that I work from that vantage point. There obviously wouldn't be any conflict if the doctor in question saw the death penalty as something positive. If your friend believes that capital punishment is ethical, his professional contribution to the practice would not contradict anything, except your own opposing opinion.

But your query suggests something murkier.

Let's assume that this doctor believes capital punishment to be ethically wrong — but he knows it will still happen regardless of his involvement. He realizes that people will be put to death one way or another, and that without his personal oversight the procedure might be conducted inhumanely. So the real question is this: Is it acceptable to participate in something unethical if the act itself is inevitable?

At least in this instance, I would say no.

We are all citizens of the same world — and it's a world that is (quite often) wicked. Unethical acts happen constantly, and most of them are outside the control of any one person. Some of them are so embedded in other activities that they are almost impossible to avoid; others are debatable or difficult to detect. But sometimes an unethical act is isolated, tangible and clear. And when this is the case, the most ethical response is to avoid participation. If there isn't a collective or legal obligation to participate, every person retains the right to opt out of activities that he sees as morally wrong. If this doctor believes that capital punishment is unethical, he should not use its inevitability as a pragmatic rationalization for his personal involvement. By overseeing the event, he is latently justifying the existence of the process.

But here's where things gets complicated: Our doctor's argument for overseeing a form of punishment he (theoretically) abhors would probably fall somewhere along these lines: "If everyone who disagreed with lethal injection removed themselves from its application, the only people policing it would be those who think lethal injection is awesome — and people like that might not care about the welfare of those sentenced to experience it." This argument is not terrible. But it doesn't hold up to scrutiny. What it ultimately suggests is that society must somehow ensure that the various details of an unethical process are nonetheless conducted as ethically as possible. Here again, the process is latently justified: Attempts to govern and humanize the procedure distract from the fact that society is consciously taking someone's life.

I'm not going to pretend that this is an easy question. It's not — in fact, each rereading of my response makes me tempted to alter my position. But my central belief is that trying to police society at large is a less reasonable aspiration than policing the day-to-day ethics of one's own life. The only thing we can truly control is how we live. As such, I think a doctor who disagrees with the death penalty should not involve himself with the practice of executions, even if his motive is humanitarian. It is a losing game.

CHAPTER 8

Perspectives From the Bench

While legislatures enact laws on the methods of capital punishment and the scope of its use, it is the courts that have become the battleground for the arguments between advocates and detractors of the death penalty. Indeed, decades of Supreme Court decisions have been responsible for curbing the death penalty, a trend often criticized as "legislating from the bench." This chapter contains excerpts from Supreme Court justices' decisions, as printed in The Times.

Blackmun: 'I . . . Concede That the Death Penalty Experiment Has Failed'

SPECIAL TO THE NEW YORK TIMES | FEB. 23, 1994

Following are excerpts from Justice Harry A. Blackmun's opinion dissenting from the Supreme Court's order denying review in a Texas death penalty case. The order, Callins v. Collins, No. 93-7054, was unsigned and was issued without an opinion.

ON FEB. 23, 1994, at approximately 1 A.M., Bruce Edwin Callins will be executed by the State of Texas. Intravenous tubes attached to his arms will carry the instrument of death, a toxic fluid designed specifically for the purpose of killing human beings. The witnesses, standing a few feet away, will behold Callins, no longer a defendant, an appellant or a petitioner, but a man, strapped to a gurney, and seconds away from extinction.

PAUL HOSEFROS/THE NEW YORK TIMES

Justice Harry A. Blackmun.

Within days, or perhaps hours, the memory of Callins will begin to fade. The wheels of justice will churn again, and somewhere, another jury or another judge will have the unenviable task of determining whether some human being is to live or die.

We hope, of course, that the defendant whose life is at risk will be represented by competent counsel, someone who is inspired by the awareness that a less-than-vigorous defense truly could have fatal consequences for the defendant. We hope that the attorney will investigate all aspects of the case, follow all evidentiary and procedural rules, and appear before a judge who is still committed to the protection of defendants' rights even now, as the prospect of meaningful judicial oversight has diminished. In the same vein, we hope that the prosecution, in urging the penalty of death, will have exercised its discretion wisely, free from bias, prejudice or political motive, and will be humbled, rather than emboldened, by the awesome authority conferred by the State.

But even if we can feel confident that these actors will fulfill their roles to the best of their human ability, our collective conscience will remain uneasy. Twenty years have passed since this Court declared that the death penalty must be imposed fairly, and with reasonable consistency or not at all (see Furman v. Georgia, 1972), and, despite the effort of the states and courts to devise legal formulas and procedural rules to meet this daunting challenge, the death penalty remains fraught with arbitrariness, discrimination, caprice and mistake.

2 CONFLICTING PRINCIPLES

This is not to say that the problems with the death penalty today are identical to those that were present 20 years ago. Rather, the problems that were pursued down one hole with procedural rules and verbal formulas have come to the surface somewhere else, just as virulent and pernicious as they were in their original form. Experience has taught us that the constitutional goal of eliminating arbitrariness and discrimination from the administration of death...can never be achieved without compromising an equally essential component of fundamental fairness: individualized sentencing. (See Lockett v. Ohio, 1978.)

It is tempting, when faced with conflicting constitutional commands, to sacrifice one for the other or to assume that an acceptable balance between them already has been struck. In the context of the death penalty, however, such jurisprudential maneuvers are wholly inappropriate. The death penalty must be imposed "fairly, and with reasonable consistency, or not at all." (Eddings v. Oklahoma, 1982.)

To be fair, a capital sentencing scheme must treat each person convicted of a capital offense with that "degree of respect due the uniqueness of the individual...." That means affording the sentencer the power and discretion to grant mercy in a particular case, and providing avenues for the consideration of any and all relevant mitigating evidence that would justify a sentence less than death.

Reasonable consistency, on the other hand, requires that the death penalty be inflicted evenhandedly, in accordance with reason and objective standards, rather than by whim, caprice or prejudice.

Finally, because human error is inevitable and because our criminal justice system is less than perfect, searching appellate review of death sentences and their underlying convictions is a prerequisite to a constitutional death penalty scheme.

'EXPERIMENT HAS FAILED'

On their face, these goals of individual fairness, reasonable consistency and absence of error appear to be attainable: Courts are in the very business of erecting procedural devices from which fair, equitable and reliable outcomes are presumed to flow. Yet, in the death penalty area, this Court, in my view, has engaged in a futile effort to balance these constitutional demands, and now is retreating not only from the Furman promise of consistency and rationality, but from the requirement of individualized sentencing as well.

Having virtually conceded that both fairness and rationality cannot be achieved in the administration of the death penalty (McCleskey v.

Kemp, 1987), the Court has chosen to deregulate the entire enterprise, replacing, it would seem, substantive constitutional requirements with mere aesthetics, and abdicating its statutorily and constitutionally imposed duty to provide meaningful judicial oversight to the administration of death by the states.

From this day forward, I no longer shall tinker with the machinery of death. For more than 20 years I have endeavored — indeed, I have struggled, along with a majority of this Court — to develop procedural and substantive rules that would lend more than the mere appearance of fairness to the death penalty endeavor.... Rather than continue to coddle the Court's delusion that the desired level of fairness has been achieved and the need for regulation eviscerated, I feel morally and intellectually obligated simply to concede that the death penalty experiment has failed. It is virtually self-evident to me now that no combination of procedural rules or substantive regulations ever can save the death penalty from its inherent constitutional deficiencies. The basic question — does the system accurately and consistently determine which defendants "deserve" to die? — cannot be answered in the affirmative.... The problem is that the inevitability of factual, legal and moral error gives us a system that we know must wrongly kill some defendants, a system that fails to deliver the fair, consistent and reliable sentences of death required by the Constitution....

DEFINING WHO DESERVES DEATH

There is little doubt now that Furman's essential holding was correct. Although most of the public seems to desire, and the Constitution appears to permit, the penalty of death, it surely is beyond dispute that if the death penalty cannot be administered consistently and rationally, it may not be administered at all....

Delivering on the Furman promise, however, has proved to be another matter. Furman aspired to eliminate the vestiges of racism and the effects of poverty in capital sentencing; it deplored the "wanton" and "random" infliction of death by a government with constitutionally limited power. Furman demanded that the sentencer's discretion be directed and limited by procedural rules and objective standards in order to minimize the risk of arbitrary and capricious sentences of death.

In the years following Furman, serious efforts were made to comply with its mandate. State legislatures and appellate courts struggled to provide judges and juries with sensible and objective guidelines for determining who should live and who should die. Some states attempted to define who is "deserving" of the death penalty through the use of carefully chosen adjectives, reserving the death penalty for those who commit crimes that are "especially heinous, atrocious or cruel," or "wantonly vile, horrible or inhuman." Other states enacted mandatory death penalty statutes, reading Furman as an invitation to eliminate sentencer discretion altogether....

FAIRNESS VS. CONSISTENCY

Unfortunately, all this experimentation and ingenuity yielded little of what Furman demanded. It soon became apparent that discretion could not be eliminated from capital sentencing without threatening the fundamental fairness due a defendant when life is at stake. Just as contemporary society was no longer tolerant of the random or discriminatory infliction of the penalty of death...evolving standards of decency required due consideration of the uniqueness of each individual defendant when imposing society's ultimate penalty.

This development in the American conscience would have presented no constitutional dilemma if fairness to the individual could be achieved without sacrificing the consistency and rationality promised in Furman. But over the past two decades, efforts to balance these competing constitutional commands have been to no avail. Experience has shown that the consistency and rationality promised in Furman are inversely related to the fairness owed the individual when considering a sentence of death. A step toward consistency is a step away from fairness....

While one might hope that providing the sentencer with as much relevant mitigating evidence as possible will lead to more rational and consistent sentences, experience has taught otherwise. It seems that the decision whether a human being should live or die is so inherently subjective, rife with all of life's understandings, experiences, prejudices and passions, that it inevitably defies the rationality and consistency required by the Constitution....

'ADMIT THE FUTILITY'

The consistency promised in Furman and the fairness to the individual demanded in Lockett are not only inversely related, but irreconcilable in the context of capital punishment. Any statute or procedure that could effectively eliminate arbitrariness from the administration of death would also restrict the sentencer's discretion to such an extent that the sentencer would be unable to give full consideration to the unique characteristics of each defendant and the circumstances of the offense.

By the same token, any statute or procedure that would provide the sentencer with sufficient discretion to consider fully and act upon the unique circumstances of each defendant would "thro(w) open the back door to arbitrary and irrational sentencing."...

In my view, the proper course when faced with irreconcilable constitutional commands is not to ignore one or the other, nor to pretend that the dilemma does not exist, but to admit the futility of the effort to harmonize them. This means accepting the fact that the death penalty cannot be administered in accord with our Constitution....

Perhaps one day this Court will develop procedural rules or verbal formulas that actually will provide consistency, fairness and reliability in a capital-sentencing scheme. I am not optimistic that such a day will come. I am more optimistic, though, that this Court eventually will conclude that the effort to eliminate arbitrariness while preserving fairness "in the infliction of (death) is so plainly doomed to failure that it and the death penalty must be abandoned altogether." (Godfrey

v. Georgia, 1980….) I may not live to see that day, but I have faith that eventually it will arrive. The path the Court has chosen lessens us all. I dissent.

Scalia: Fifth Amendment 'Clearly Permits the Death Penalty'

SPECIAL TO THE NEW YORK TIMES | FEB. 23, 1994

Following are excerpts from Justice Antonin Scalia's opinion concurring in the Supreme Court's order denying review in a Texas death penalty case, Callins v. Collins, No. 93-7054. In it, Justice Scalia responds to Justice Harry A. Blackmun's condemnation of the death penalty.

JUSTICE BLACKMUN DISSENTS from the denial of certiorari in this case with a statement explaining why the death penalty "as currently administered," is contrary to the Constitution of the United States. That explanation often refers to "intellectual, moral and personal" perceptions, but never to the text and tradition of the Constitution. It is the latter rather than the former that ought to control. The Fifth Amendment provides that "(n)o person shall be held to answer for a capital... crime, unless on a presentment or indictment of a Grand Jury,...nor be deprived of life...without due process of law." This clearly permits the death penalty to be imposed, and establishes beyond doubt that the death penalty is not one of the "cruel and unusual punishments" prohibited by the Eighth Amendment.

As Justice Blackmun describes, however, over the years since 1972 this Court has attached to the imposition of the death penalty two quite incompatible sets of commands: the sentencer's discretion to impose death must be closely confined (see Furman v. Georgia, 1972), but the sentencer's discretion not to impose death (to extend mercy) must be unlimited (Eddings v. Oklahoma, 1982; Lockett v. Ohio 1978). These commands were invented without benefit of any textual or historical support; they are the product of just such "intellectual, moral and personal" perceptions as Justice Blackmun expresses today, some of which...have been made part of what is called "the Court's Eighth Amendment jurisprudence."

Though Justice Blackmun joins those of us who have acknowledged the incompatibility of the Court's Furman and Lockett-Eddings lines of jurisprudence...he unfortunately draws the wrong conclusion from the acknowledgment....

Surely a different conclusion commends itself to wit, that at least one of these judicially announced irreconcilable commands which cause the Constitution to prohibit what its text explicitly permits must be wrong.

Convictions in opposition to the death penalty are often passionate and deeply held. That would be no excuse for reading them into a Constitution that does not contain them, even if they represented the convictions of a majority of Americans. Much less is there any excuse for using that course to thrust a minority's views upon the people.

Justice Blackmun begins his statement by describing with poignancy the death of a convicted murderer by lethal injection. He chooses, as the case in which to make that statement, one of the less brutal of the murders that regularly come before us, the murder of a man ripped by a bullet suddenly and unexpectedly, with no opportunity to prepare himself and his affairs, and left to bleed to death on the floor of a tavern. The death-by-injection which Justice Blackmun describes looks pretty desirable next to that.

It looks even better next to some of the other cases currently before us, which Justice Blackmun did not select as the vehicle for his announcement that the death penalty is always unconstitutional, for example, the case of the 11-year-old girl raped by four men and then killed by stuffing her panties down her throat....How enviable a quiet death by lethal injection compared with that!

If the people conclude that such more brutal deaths may be deterred by capital punishment; indeed, if they merely conclude that justice requires such brutal deaths to be avenged by capital punishment; the creation of false, untextual and unhistorical contradictions within "the Court's Eighth Amendment jurisprudence" should not prevent them.

Excerpts From Ruling and Dissent on Who Decides the Death Penalty

BY THE NEW YORK TIMES | JUNE 25, 2002

Following are excerpts from the Supreme Court's ruling today that juries, not judges, must make the crucial factual determinations that make a convicted murderer eligible for the death penalty. The vote in Ring v. Arizona was 7 to 2. Justice Ruth Bader Ginsburg wrote the majority opinion, in which Justices Antonin Scalia, Stephen G. Breyer, Anthony M. Kennedy, Clarence Thomas, David M. Souter and John Paul Stevens concurred. Justice Sandra Day O'Connor wrote the dissent, in which Chief Justice William H. Rehnquist joined.

FROM THE DECISION

By Justice Ginsburg

THIS CASE CONCERNS the Sixth Amendment right to a jury trial in capital prosecutions. In Arizona, following a jury adjudication of a defendant's guilt of first-degree murder, the trial judge, sitting alone, determines the presence or absence of the aggravating factors required by Arizona law for imposition of the death penalty.

In Walton v. Arizona (1990), this Court held that Arizona's sentencing scheme was compatible with the Sixth Amendment because the additional facts found by the judge qualified as sentencing considerations, not as "elements of the offense of capital murder." Ten years later, however, we decided Apprendi v. New Jersey (2000), which held that the Sixth Amendment does not permit a defendant to be "exposed...to a penalty exceeding the maximum he would receive if punished according to the facts reflected in the jury verdict alone." This prescription governs, Apprendi determined, even if the state characterizes the additional findings made by the judge as "sentencing factors." Apprendi's reasoning is irreconcilable with Walton's holding in this regard, and today we overrule Walton in relevant part. Capital defendants, no less than non-capital defendants, we conclude, are entitled to a jury determination of any fact on which the legislature conditions an increase in their maximum punishment.

At the trial of petitioner Timothy Ring for murder, armed robbery, and related charges, the prosecutor presented evidence sufficient to permit the jury to find the facts here recounted. On Nov. 28, 1994, a Wells Fargo armored van pulled up to the Dillard's department store at Arrowhead Mall in Glendale, Ariz. Courier Dave Moss left the van to pick up money inside the store. When he returned, the van, and its driver, John Magoch, were gone.

Later that day, Maricopa County Sheriff's Deputies found the van — its doors locked and its engine running — in the parking lot of a church in Sun City, Ariz. Inside the vehicle they found Magoch, dead from a single gunshot to the head. According to Wells Fargo records, more than $562,000 in cash and $271,000 in checks were missing from the van.

Prompted by an informant's tip, Glendale police sought to determine whether Ring and his friend James Greenham were involved in the robbery....Under Arizona law, Ring could not be sentenced to death, the statutory maximum penalty for first-degree murder, unless further findings were made. The state's first-degree murder statute prescribes that the offense "is punishable by death or life imprisonment as provided by 13-703." The cross-referenced section, 13-703, directs the judge who presided at trial to "conduct a separate sentencing hearing to determine the existence or nonexistence of [certain enumerated] circumstances...for the purpose of determining the sentence to be imposed."

The statute further instructs: "The hearing shall be conducted before the court alone. The court alone shall make all factual determinations required by this section or the Constitution of the United States or this state."

At the conclusion of the sentencing hearing, the judge is to determine the presence or absence of the enumerated "aggravating circumstances" and any "mitigating circumstances." The state's law authorizes the judge to sentence the defendant to death only if there is at least one aggravating circumstance and "there are no mitigating circumstances sufficiently substantial to call for leniency."...On Oct. 29, 1997, the trial judge entered his "Special Verdict" sentencing Ring to death. Because Ring was convicted of felony murder, not premeditated murder, the judge recognized that Ring was eligible for the death penalty only if he was Magoch's actual killer or if he was "a major participant in the armed robbery that led to the killing and exhibited a reckless disregard or indifference for human life."

Citing Greenham's testimony at the sentencing hearing, the judge concluded that Ring "is the one who shot and killed Mr. Magoch." The judge also found that Ring was a major participant in the robbery and that armed robbery "is unquestionably a crime which carries with it a grave risk of death."

The judge then turned to the determination of aggravating and mitigating circumstances. He found two aggravating factors. First, the judge determined that Ring committed the offense in expectation of receiving something of "pecuniary value," as described in 13-703. Second, the judge found that the offense was committed "in an especially heinous, cruel or depraved manner." In support of this finding, he cited Ring's comment, as reported by Greenham at the sentencing hearing, expressing pride in his marksmanship. The judge found one nonstatutory mitigating factor: Ring's "minimal" criminal record. In his judgment, that mitigating circumstance did not "call for leniency"; he therefore sentenced Ring to death.

On appeal, Ring argued that Arizona's capital sentencing scheme violates the Sixth and Fourteenth Amendments to the U.S. Constitution because it entrusts to a judge the finding of a fact raising the defendant's maximum penalty. The state, in response, noted that this Court had upheld Arizona's system in Walton v. Arizona (1990), and had stated in Apprendi that Walton remained good law....

Although it agreed with the Apprendi dissent's reading of Arizona law, the Arizona court understood that it was bound by the Supremacy Clause to apply Walton, which this Court had not overruled. It therefore rejected Ring's constitutional attack on the state's capital murder judicial sentencing system.

The court agreed with Ring that the evidence was insufficient to support the aggravating circumstance of depravity, but it upheld the trial court's finding on the aggravating factor of pecuniary gain. The Arizona Supreme Court then reweighed that remaining factor against the sole mitigating circumstance (Ring's lack of a serious criminal record), and affirmed the death sentence.

We granted Ring's petition for a writ of certiorari, to allay uncertainty in the lower courts caused by the manifest tension between Walton and the reasoning of Apprendi. We now reverse the judgment of the Arizona Supreme Court.

Based solely on the jury's verdict finding Ring guilty of first-degree felony murder, the maximum punishment he could have received was life imprisonment. This was so because, in Arizona, a "death sentence may not legally be imposed...unless at least one aggravating factor is found to exist beyond a reasonable doubt." The question presented is whether that aggravating factor may be found by the judge, as Arizona law specifies, or whether the Sixth Amendment's jury trial guarantee, made applicable to the states by the Fourteenth Amendment, requires that the aggravating factor determination be entrusted to the jury....

In an effort to reconcile its capital sentencing system with the Sixth Amendment as interpreted by Apprendi, Arizona first restates the Apprendi majority's portrayal of Arizona's system: Ring was convicted of first-degree murder, for which Arizona law specifies "death or life imprisonment" as the only sentencing options, Ring was therefore sentenced within the range of punishment authorized by the jury verdict. This argument overlooks Apprendi's instruction that "the relevant inquiry is one not of form, but of effect."

In effect, "the required finding [of an aggravated circumstance] exposed [Ring] to a greater punishment than that authorized by the jury's guilty verdict." The Arizona first-degree murder statute "authorizes a maximum penalty of death only in a formal sense," for it explicitly cross-references the statutory provision requiring the finding of an aggravating circumstance before imposition of the death penalty. If Arizona prevailed on its opening argument, Apprendi would be reduced to a "meaningless and formalistic" rule of statutory drafting....

In any event, the superiority of judicial fact finding in capital cases is far from evident. Unlike Arizona, the great majority of states responded to this Court's Eighth Amendment decisions requiring the presence of aggravating circumstances in capital cases by entrusting those determinations to the jury. Although " 'the doctrine of stare decisis is of fundamental importance to the rule of law,'...our precedents are not sacrosanct." "We have overruled prior decisions where the necessity and propriety of doing so has been established." We are satisfied that this is such a case....

For the reasons stated, we hold that Walton and Apprendi are irreconcilable; our Sixth Amendment jurisprudence cannot be home to both. Accordingly, we overrule Walton to the extent that it allows a sentencing judge, sitting without a jury, to find an aggravating circumstance necessary for imposition of the death penalty. Because Arizona's enumerated aggravating factors operate as "the functional equivalent of an element of a greater offense," the Sixth Amendment requires that they be found by a jury....

The right to trial by jury guaranteed by the Sixth Amendment would be senselessly diminished if it encompassed the fact finding necessary to increase a defendant's sentence by two years, but not the fact finding necessary to put him to death. We hold that the Sixth Amendment applies to both.

FROM THE DISSENT

By Justice O'Connor

I understand why the Court holds that the reasoning of Apprendi v. New Jersey is irreconcilable with Walton v. Arizona. Yet in choosing which to overrule, I would choose Apprendi, not Walton.

I continue to believe, for the reasons I articulated in my dissent in Apprendi, that the decision in Apprendi was a serious mistake. As I argued in that dissent, Apprendi's rule that any fact that increases the maximum penalty must be treated as an element of the crime is not required by the Constitution, by history, or by our prior cases. Indeed, the rule directly contradicts several of our prior cases. And it ignores the "significant history in this country of...discretionary sentencing by judges." The Court has failed, both in Apprendi and in the decision announced today, to "offer any meaningful justification for deviating from years of cases both suggesting and holding that application of the 'increase in the maximum penalty' rule is not required by the Constitution."

Not only was the decision in Apprendi unjustified in my view, but it has also had a severely destabilizing effect on our criminal justice system. I predicted in my dissent that the decision would "unleash a flood of petitions by convicted defendants seeking to invalidate their sentences in whole or in part on the authority of [Apprendi]." As of May 31, 2002, less than two years after Apprendi was announced, the United States Courts of Appeals had decided approximately 1,802 criminal appeals in which defendants challenged their sentences, and in some cases even their convictions, under Apprendi.

These federal appeals are likely only the tip of the iceberg, as federal criminal prosecutions represent a tiny fraction of the total number of criminal prosecutions nationwide. The number of second or successive habeas corpus petitions filed in the federal courts also increased by 77 percent in 2001, a phenomenon the Administrative Office of the United States Courts attributes to prisoners bringing Apprendi claims.

This Court has been similarly overwhelmed by the aftershocks of Apprendi. A survey of the petitions for certiorari we received in the past year indicates that 18 percent raised Apprendi-related claims. It is simply beyond dispute that Apprendi threw countless criminal sentences into doubt and thereby caused an enormous increase in the workload of an already overburdened judiciary.

The decision today is only going to add to these already serious effects. The Court effectively declares five states' capital sentencing schemes unconstitutional. (Colorado, Idaho, Montana, Nebraska and Arizona.) There are 168 prisoners on death row in these states, each of whom is now likely to challenge his or her death sentence. I believe many of these challenges will ultimately be unsuccessful, either because the prisoners will be unable to satisfy the standards of harmless error or plain error review, or because, having completed their direct appeals, they will be barred from taking advantage of today's holding on federal collateral review.

Nonetheless, the need to evaluate these claims will greatly burden the courts in these five states. In addition, I fear that the prisoners on death row in Alabama, Delaware, Florida and Indiana, which the Court identifies as having hybrid sentencing schemes in which the jury renders an advisory verdict but the judge makes the ultimate sentencing determination....

By expanding on Apprendi, the Court today exacerbates the harm done in that case. Consistent with my dissent, I would overrule Apprendi rather than Walton.

FROM THE CONCURRENCE

By Justice Scalia

The question whether Walton v. Arizona (1990) survives our decision in Apprendi v. New Jersey (2000) confronts me with a difficult choice. What compelled Arizona (and many other states) to specify particular "aggravating factors" that must be found before the death penalty can be imposed was the line of this Court's cases beginning with Furman v. Georgia (1972). In my view, that line of decisions had no proper foundation in the Constitution. I am therefore reluctant to magnify the burdens that our Furman jurisprudence imposes on the States. Better for the Court to have invented an evidentiary requirement that a judge can find by a preponderance of the evidence, than to invent one that a unanimous jury must find beyond a reasonable doubt.

On the other hand, as I wrote in my dissent in Almendarez-Torres v. United States (1998), and as reaffirmed by joining the opinion for the Court in Apprendi, I believe that the fundamental meaning of the jury-trial guarantee of the Sixth Amendment is that all facts essential to imposition of the level of punishment that the defendant receives — whether the statute calls them elements of the offense, sentencing factors or Mary Jane — must be found by the jury beyond a reasonable doubt....

My observing over the past 12 years the accelerating propensity of both state and federal legislatures to adopt "sentencing factors" determined by judges that increase punishment beyond what is authorized by the jury's verdict, and my witnessing the belief of a near majority of my colleagues that this novel practice is perfectly O.K., cause me to believe that our people's traditional belief in the right of trial by jury is in perilous decline. That decline is bound to be confirmed, and indeed accelerated, by the repeated spectacle of a man's going to his death because a judge found that an aggravating factor existed. We cannot preserve our veneration for the protection of the jury in criminal cases if we render ourselves callous to the need for that protection by regularly imposing the death penalty without it.

FROM THE CONCURRENCE

By Justice Breyer

Given my views in Apprendi v. New Jersey (dissenting opinion) and Harris v. United States, I cannot join the Court's opinion. I concur in the judgment, however, because I believe that jury sentencing in capital cases is mandated by the Eighth Amendment....

Even in jurisdictions where judges are selected directly by the people, the jury remains uniquely capable of determining whether, given the community's views, capital punishment is appropriate in the particular case at hand.

The importance of trying to translate a community's sense of capital punishment's appropriateness in a particular case is underscored

DAMON WINTER/THE NEW YORK TIMES

Supreme Court Justice Stephen Breyer, photographed at his home in Cambridge, Mass., on Sept. 3, 2015.

by the continued division of opinion as to whether capital punishment is in all circumstances, as currently administered, "cruel and unusual." Those who make this claim point, among other things, to the fact that death is not reversible, and to death sentences imposed upon those whose convictions proved unreliable.

They point to the potentially arbitrary application of the death penalty, adding that the race of the victim and socioeconomic factors seem to matter. They argue that the delays that increasingly accompany sentences of death make those sentences unconstitutional because of "the suffering inherent in a prolonged wait for execution."

They point to the inadequacy of representation in capital cases, a fact that aggravates the other failings.

And they note that other nations have increasingly abandoned capital punishment.

Many communities may have accepted some or all of these claims, for they do not impose capital sentences. Leaving questions of arbitrariness aside, this diversity argues strongly for procedures that will help assure that, in a particular case, the community indeed believes application of the death penalty is appropriate, not "cruel," "unusual," or otherwise unwarranted.

For these reasons, the danger of unwarranted imposition of the penalty cannot be avoided unless "the decision to impose the death penalty is made by a jury rather than by a single governmental official." And I conclude that the Eighth Amendment requires individual jurors to make, and to take responsibility for, a decision to sentence a person to death.

CHAPTER 9

Lethal Injection and the Death Penalty Today

In 1982, Texas became the first state to execute an inmate by lethal injection. Since then, it has become the most common method of execution nationwide. Its supporters argue that, when administered correctly, it is the most painless form of execution. However, opponents have challenged the administration of such drugs by untrained prison staff as well as states' secrecy regarding how such drugs are obtained, pointing to numerous botched executions as proof of the cruelty of lethal injection.

Technician Executes Murderer in Texas by Lethal Injection

BY ROBERT REINHOLD | DEC. 7, 1982

THE STATE OF TEXAS injected Charles Brooks Jr. with a deadly combination of sedatives and drugs just after midnight today, making him the first condemned prisoner in the United States to die by lethal injection.

The lethal drugs were injected into Mr. Brooks's body at 12:09 A.M. At 12:16, he was pronounced dead by a prison doctor. The execution took place at the state prison here after a day of frantic legal appeals for the 40-year-old prisoner had failed. Neither the United States Supreme Court nor Gov. William Clements saw merit to the pleas for a reprieve. The Supreme Court voted 6 to 3 to reject the petition for a stay.

According to four reporters who witnessed the execution, Mr. Brooks was rolled into the death chamber on a stretcher. He looked up at his girlfriend, Vanessa Sapp, and said, "I love you."

The reporters said Mr. Brooks, who had converted to the Moslem faith, also uttered some prayers, among them, "I bear witness there is no God but Allah. I bear witness that Mohammed is the messenger of God."

The witnesses, all of whom appeared shaken by the experience, indicated that Mr. Brooks's death did not appear to be painless. Dick Reavis, a reporter for Texas Monthly, said, "He turned his head upward and yawned, then wheezed, and that was all," but another witness said Mr. Brooks gasped and moved his stomach.

There were about 20 witnesses in the death chamber, three of them invited by Mr. Brooks. One of them, a black Muslim minister from Fort Worth, Larry Amin Sherrief, said that the prisoner had come to recognize "it is the Lord's will, and he will abide by it."

Mr. Brooks had been sentenced to die for his role in the 1976 murder of David Gregory, a Fort Worth automobile mechanic who was bound and shot once through the head after Mr. Brooks and an accomplice, Woody Lourdes, stole a car in which Mr. Gregory accompanied them on a "test ride" in 1976.

The lethal liquid was injected through a vein in his arm by a medical technician on the other side of a wall through which tubes had been passed.

Mr. Brooks was the first black man to die by execution since 1967. He was said to have been resigned to the execution. He offered little resistance when taken to the death chamber at the old red-brick Walls unit of the prison complex.

Because of legal complications, Mr. Brooks's accomplice, Mr. Lourdes, is serving a 40-year term for the crime. Mr. Brooks's lawyers, and even the prosecutor who obtained his conviction, had maintained that the disparity in the two sentences, for the same crime, was unjust. Even though only one shot was fired, the state was never able to determine which man pulled the trigger. Neither of the two would say.

The use of lethal injection has been widely urged as a "humane" way of carrying out the death sentence. However, many physicians have protested that it is a violation of medical ethics to use drugs meant to save lives in order to end lives. On Monday, the medical director of the Texas prison system said he and his staff had assisted in preparations for the execution.

The remarks of Dr. Ralph Gray, medical director of the Texas Department of Correction, seemed likely to stir intense debate among physicians. Prison authorities, however, had said that apart from pronouncing the prisoner dead, no doctors were to be involved in the execution.

In a telephone interview Monday from his office here in Huntsville, Dr. Gray said he had visited the prisoner on death row this morning to see if his veins were large enough to accept the catheter needle through which a deadly barbiturate, sodium thiopental, would be introduced.

"He's got plenty of good veins — that's why I went over to see him," Dr. Gray said. He also indicated that the barbiturate would be taken from prison drug supplies under his control and that some of the medical technicians trained to perform the execution were members of the prison health staff.

BOARD REFUSES A STAY

In New Orleans, the United States Court of Appeals for the Fifth Circuit refused to issue a stay. This afternoon the State Board of Pardons and Paroles recommended, by a vote of 2 to 1, that the execution proceed.

Five men, all white, have been executed since the Supreme Court allowed executions to go forward again in 1976 after a decade's hiatus. In all, according to Henry Schwarzchild, director of the capital punishment project of the American Civil Liberties Union, about 1,150 inmates are awaiting execution in the 37 states that permit the death penalty.

The last execution in Texas took place in 1964. The state, with about 160 condemned prisoners, has more people awaiting execution than any state except Florida, with 200. New York has no death penalty. New Jersey re-adopoted the punishment in August. Governor Kean asked the Legislature for an additional measure to permit execution by injection as "the most humane form" of death.

PRISONERS GIVEN AN OPTION

Beside Texas, four states now prescribe or permit execution by injection: Oklahoma, Idaho, New Mexico and Washington. In Idaho, the law specifies that the prison warden can elect to use a firing squad should the injection method prove unworkable. In Washington the condemned prisoner may elect to be hanged.

Mr. Brooks was generally considered bright and personable. He was raised by a comparatively well-off family in Fort Worth, the son of the late Charles Brooks Sr., who held a well-paying job at a meatpacking company in Fort Worth. The father reportedly lavished presents and affection on his son. The boy was a star football player and popular personality at I.M. Terrell High School. The younger Mr. Brooks married his high-school sweetheart and fathered two sons, now in college.

Cruel and Unusual History

OPINION | BY GILBERT KING | APRIL 23, 2008

THE SUPREME COURT concluded last week, in a 7-2 ruling, that Kentucky's three-drug method of execution by lethal injection does not violate the Eighth Amendment's prohibition on cruel and unusual punishment. In his plurality opinion, Chief Justice John Roberts cited a Supreme Court principle from a ruling in 1890 that defines cruelty as limited to punishments that "involve torture or a lingering death."

But the court was wrong in the 19th century, an error that has infected its jurisprudence for more than 100 years. In this nation's landmark capital punishment cases, the resultant executions were anything but free from torture and prolonged deaths.

The first of those landmark cases, the 1879 case of Wilkerson v. Utah, was cited by Justice Clarence Thomas, in his concurring opinion in the Kentucky case. The court "had no difficulty concluding that death by firing squad" did not amount to cruel and unusual punishment, Justice Thomas wrote.

Wallace Wilkerson might have begged to differ. Once the Supreme Court affirmed Utah's right to eradicate him by rifle, Wilkerson was let into a jailyard where he declined to be blindfolded. A sheriff gave the command to fire and Wilkerson braced for the barrage. He moved just enough for the bullets to strike his arm and torso but not his heart.

"My God!" Wilkerson shrieked. "My God! They have missed!" More than 27 minutes passed as Wilkerson bled to death in front of astonished witnesses and a helpless doctor.

Just 11 years later, the Supreme Court heard the case of William Kemmler, who had been sentenced to death by electric chair in New York. The court, in affirming the state's right to execute Kemmler, ruled that electrocution reduced substantial risks of pain or "a lingering death" when compared to executions by hanging. Kemmler, had he lived through the ensuing execution (and he nearly did), might too have disagreed.

After a thousand volts of current struck Kemmler on Aug. 6, 1890, the smell of burnt flesh permeated the room. He was still breathing. Saliva dripped from his mouth and down his beard as he gasped for air. Nauseated witnesses and a tearful sheriff fled the room as Kemmler's coat burst into flames.

Another surge was applied, but minutes passed as the current built to a lethal voltage. Some witnesses thought Kemmler was about to regain consciousness, but eight long minutes later, he was pronounced dead.

Perhaps the most egregious case came to the court more than 50 years later. "Lucky" Willie Francis, as the press called him, was a stuttering 17-year-old from St. Martinville, La. In 1946, he walked away from the electric chair known as "Gruesome Gertie" when two executioners (an inmate and a guard) from the state penitentiary at Angola botched the wiring of the chair.

When the switch was thrown, Francis strained against the straps and began rocking and sliding in the chair, pleading with the sheriff and the executioners to halt the proceedings. "I am n-n-not dying!" he screamed. Gov. Jimmie Davis ordered Francis returned to the chair six days later.

Francis' lawyers obtained a stay, and the case reached the Supreme Court. Justice Felix Frankfurter defined the teenager's ordeal as an "innocent misadventure." In the decision, Louisiana ex rel. Francis v. Resweber, the court held that "accidents happen for which no man is to blame," and that such "an accident, with no suggestion of malevolence" did not violate the Constitution.

Fewer than 24 hours before Francis' second scheduled execution, his lawyers tried to bring the case before the Supreme Court again. They had obtained affidavits from witnesses stating that the two executioners from Angola were, as one of the witnesses put it, "so drunk it would have been impossible for them to have known what they were doing." Although the court rejected this last-minute appeal, it noted

BETTMANN/GETTY IMAGES

Willie Francis survived a botched execution on May 3, 1946. After the Supreme Court rejected his appeal, he was executed a year later at age 18.

the "grave nature of the new allegations" and encouraged the lawyers to pursue the matter in state court first, as required by law.

Willie Francis was executed the next morning. Because his case never made it back to the Supreme Court, the ruling lingers, influencing the decisions of today's justices. In his plurality opinion last week, Chief Justice Roberts called Louisiana's first attempt at executing Francis an "isolated mishap" that "while regrettable, does not suggest cruelty."

Justice Clarence Thomas, writing separately, also mentioned the Francis case: "No one suggested that Louisiana was required to implement additional safeguards or alternative procedures in order to reduce the risk of a second malfunction." In fact, Louisiana did just that. Two weeks after the botched execution of Willie Francis, its Legislature required that the operator of the electric chair "shall be a competent electrician who shall not have been previously convicted of a felony." This law would have prohibited both executioners from participating in Francis' failed execution.

The court's majority opinion in the Willie Francis case acknowledged, "The traditional humanity of modern Anglo-American law forbids the infliction of unnecessary pain in the execution of the death sentence." Yet the Supreme Court continues to flout that standard.

In its ruling last week, the court once more ignored the consequences of its rulings for men like Wallace Wilkerson, William Kemmler and Willie Francis. The justices cited and applied Wilkerson's and Kemmler's cases as if their executions went off without a hitch.

And 60 years after two drunken executioners disregarded the tortured screams of a teenage boy named Willie Francis, the Supreme Court continues to do so.

GILBERT KING is the author of "The Execution of Willie Francis: Race, Murder and the Search for Justice in the American South."

Supreme Court Allows Lethal Injection for Execution

BY LINDA GREENHOUSE | APRIL 17, 2008

WASHINGTON — The Supreme Court on Wednesday upheld Kentucky's method of execution by lethal injection, rejecting the claim that officials there administered a common sequence of three drugs in a manner that posed an unconstitutional risk that a condemned inmate would suffer acute yet undetectable pain.

While the 7-to-2 ruling did not shut the door on challenges to the lethal injection protocols in other states, it set a standard that will not be easy to meet. Chief Justice John G. Roberts Jr. said in the court's controlling opinion that challengers must show not only that a state's method "creates a demonstrated risk of severe pain," but also that there were alternatives that were "feasible" and "readily implemented" that would "significantly" reduce that risk.

"A slightly or marginally safer alternative" would not suffice, the chief justice said. He added: "Simply because an execution method may result in pain, either by accident or as an inescapable consequence of death, does not establish the sort of 'objectively intolerable risk of harm' that qualifies as cruel and unusual" under the Eighth Amendment.

At issue in the case was not the constitutionality of lethal injection itself, the method specified by 35 of the 36 states that have the death penalty. (Nebraska is the exception.) Rather, the challenge was to the details of the injection's administration: the chemicals used, the training of the personnel, the adequacy of medical supervision, and the consequences and risk of error.

The legal question was what standard to apply in evaluating the risk. The appeal, brought by two men on Kentucky's death row, Ralph Baze and Thomas C. Bowling, each convicted of double murders, asked the court to find the Kentucky protocol unconstitutional if it imposed an "unnecessary risk" of error in light of potential alternatives. Chief

Justice Roberts, applying the more rigorous standard he outlined, said the risks identified by the inmates were not "so substantial or imminent as to amount to an Eighth Amendment violation."

While most states use a method similar to Kentucky's, a number of them have adopted additional safeguards to ensure that an inmate is properly anesthetized by the initial drug in the sequence, a barbiturate, before administration of the second two, which paralyze the muscles and stop the heart.

In fact, Justice Ruth Bader Ginsburg, in a dissenting opinion, listed several of these states and described the extra steps they have taken, to show that Kentucky could and should be required to do a better job. The states she named were Alabama, California, Florida, Indiana and Missouri. The other dissenter, Justice David H. Souter, signed her opinion.

Dozens of executions have been delayed around the country in recent months. Gov. Tim Kaine of Virginia, a Democrat, announced within hours of the ruling that he was lifting a moratorium on executions he had imposed, and other states were expected to follow. The Supreme Court itself had not imposed a general moratorium, instead granting individual stays of execution in cases that reached the court. Those stays will dissolve automatically when the justices deny the underlying appeals, as they are expected to do in the next week or two.

The court issued its decision on the same morning that it heard arguments in another closely watched death penalty case, a challenge to Louisiana's application of capital punishment for the crime of child rape. The two men on Louisiana's death row for raping young girls are the only two people in the country who have been sentenced to death for a crime in which death did not result.

In the Kentucky case, there was considerably less agreement among the justices than the vote of 7 to 2 might indicate. Six of the seven justices in the majority wrote separate opinions. The chief justice's opinion was signed by only two others, Justices Anthony M. Kennedy and Samuel A. Alito Jr. Justice Kennedy was the only member of the majority who did not write separately.

Justice Alito wrote a separate opinion suggesting that he regarded the chief justice's opinion as insufficiently conclusive and therefore open to "misinterpretation" by those who might see it as an invitation to "litigation gridlock." Justice Alito said that because ethics rules bar most medical professionals from taking part in executions, challenges based on the absence of doctors and nurses from the execution chamber must fail because an alternative protocol that would require their participation "cannot be regarded as 'feasible' or readily available."

Another member of the majority, Justice John Paul Stevens, said in his separate opinion that he felt bound by the court's precedents to uphold the constitutionality of the Kentucky protocol. But he went on to call for abolishing the death penalty, both as a matter of policy and of Eighth Amendment jurisprudence. "State-sanctioned killing," Justice Stevens said, was "becoming more and more anachronistic."

Justice Stevens voted with the majority that restored capital punishment in 1976, his first year on the court. But he said he had changed his mind, based on "my own experience" in seeing how the death penalty is actually carried out in a changing climate. Among the factors he singled out was a series of decisions that he said had "endorsed procedures that provide less protections to capital defendants than to ordinary offenders."

The set of opinions in this case, Baze v. Rees, No. 07-5439, put the personalities and priorities of the individual justices on display as much as any case in recent years.

There was Chief Justice Roberts, including in his opinion a discourse on the need for courts to step aside. The Kentucky inmates' proposed approach, he said, "would embroil the courts in ongoing scientific controversies beyond their expertise and would substantially intrude on the role of state legislatures in implementing their execution procedures."

There was Justice Stevens, the court's senior member, who turns 88 on Sunday, taking a singular path as he has so often during his long career.

There was Justice Antonin Scalia, pugnacious as ever, sufficiently provoked by Justice Stevens's position as to demand, in a separate opinion, "What prompts Justice Stevens to repudiate his prior view and to adopt the astounding position that a criminal sanction expressly mentioned in the Constitution violates the Constitution?" He added, "Purer expression cannot be found of the principle of rule by judicial fiat."

There was Justice Clarence Thomas, joining the majority judgment while expressing the view that "this is an easy case" because "a method of execution violates the Eighth Amendment only if it is deliberately designed to inflict pain," which Kentucky's protocol obviously was not.

There was another member of the majority, Justice Stephen G. Breyer, digging deeply into the scientific evidence and concluding that, while there were grounds for "legitimate concern," he could not find "either in the record or in the readily available literature that I have seen, sufficient grounds to believe that Kentucky's method of lethal injection creates a significant risk of unnecessary suffering."

And there was Justice Ginsburg, writing a carefully modulated, almost minimalist dissenting opinion in which she did not go so far as to declare Kentucky's protocol unconstitutional. Rather, she said, the court should "vacate and remand" the Kentucky Supreme Court's decision that upheld the protocol, instructing it to consider whether the state's omission of safeguards used by other states "poses an untoward, readily avoidable risk of inflicting severe and unnecessary pain."

The argument about pain is based on the sequence of drugs used by Kentucky and other states. Pancuronium bromide, which is a paralyzing agent, and potassium chloride, which stops the heart, would both cause excruciating pain if a person was not first placed under deep anesthesia. If the anesthesia is insufficient, the paralyzed inmate would not be able to move or cry out.

There have been various problems with lethal injection executions, including evidence of insufficient anesthesia in some cases. One hurdle for the Kentucky challengers was that the state has carried out only one execution, which proceeded without apparent problems, since adopting the method in 1998.

Donald B. Verrilli Jr., who argued the case for the two inmates, said in an interview that it still remained open to challengers to argue that even in a state with a protocol that looked acceptable on paper, officials were not carrying it out with sufficient care.

Immediately after announcing the lethal injection decision on Wednesday, the court turned to the argument in the Louisiana case on the constitutionality of the death penalty for raping a child.

It has been 43 years since anyone has been executed in the United States for rape. In 1977, with 30 men on death row for rape, the court ruled in a Georgia case that the Eighth Amendment prohibited the death penalty for that crime. The victim in that case, Coker v. Georgia, was a 16-year-old married woman who was referred to as an adult throughout the opinion.

While the question presented to the court in the Coker case did not differentiate between adults and children, the decision for years was widely interpreted as barring capital punishment for any rape. Nonetheless, Louisiana enacted its law in 1995, and several other states followed suit, for a current total of five that permit the death penalty for the rape of a child.

The justices' questions from the bench indicated that most saw the Coker decision as limited to adult victims, with the issue of whether death could be imposed for raping a child still an open one, not governed by precedent. Patrick Kennedy, the defendant in this case, Kennedy v. Louisiana, No. 07-343, was convicted of raping his 8-year-old stepdaughter.

Only in Louisiana could he have received the death penalty, because the other states — Montana, Oklahoma, South Carolina and Texas — apply their laws only to those with prior convictions. Mr. Kennedy's lawyer, Jeffrey L. Fisher, argued that this demonstrated a "national consensus" against the penalty, at least for a first-time offender.

Panel Urges One-Drug Lethal Injections

BY ERIK ECKHOLM | MAY 7, 2014

DAYS AFTER PRESIDENT OBAMA said a bungled execution in Oklahoma was "deeply disturbing" and called for a review of how fairly the death penalty was used, a bipartisan panel of legal experts has urged sweeping changes in what it calls the "deeply flawed" administration of capital punishment.

"I support the death penalty for guilty people but not for innocent people," said a leader of the panel, Mark White, a Democrat who oversaw 19 executions as the governor of Texas from 1983 to 1987. "We run the real risk today of executing innocent people."

The committee, which finished its report before the Oklahoma execution on April 29 and was scheduled to release it on Wednesday, is calling on states to stop using the troubled three-drug sequence commonly used for lethal injections. It said that approach carried an unacceptable risk of causing pain and suffering, as it apparently did in Oklahoma last week when an insufficiently sedated prisoner writhed and mumbled for several minutes before dying of heart failure.

Instead, the report says, executions should be carried out with large doses of a single anesthetic or barbiturate, the same method used in doctor-assisted suicides in states like Oregon.

Many medical experts agree, but an acute shortage of traditional barbiturates, mainly because manufacturers refuse to provide them for executions, has led states to scramble for secret suppliers and try out new drug combinations. Mr. White said in an interview that it was up to the states to find a humane method.

The report, "Irreversible Error," was written by experts assembled by The Constitution Project, a research and advocacy group in Washington. The panel included supporters and foes of capital punishment and was led by Mr. White, Gerald Kogan, a former chief justice of the

Florida Supreme Court, and Beth A. Wilkinson, a former federal prosecutor. It included former state attorneys general, judges and corrections officials.

Capital punishment remains available in 32 states, although the annual number of executions is in decline.

In another sign of fallout from Oklahoma's botched execution last week, lawyers for Robert James Campbell, who is scheduled to be executed on May 13 in Texas, filed a request on Tuesday for a delay, based on what they called the "unimaginably torturous conduct" in the Oklahoma execution last week of Clayton D. Lockett.

Though Texas will use one drug, in line with the Constitution Project panel's recommendation, it has kept the source secret, leading to what Mr. Campbell's lawyers called "a substantial risk that Mr. Campbell's execution could be as horrific as Mr. Lockett's."

Most of the new report focused on what the group called ongoing procedural deficiencies in the imposition of death sentences.

It called for relaxing constraints on the review of exculpatory evidence after a person has already been convicted, for federal standards for forensic laboratories and for universal videotaping of interrogations to help weed out false confessions.

It devoted considerable attention to what it called the inconsistent application of a 2002 Supreme Court ruling that the death penalty should not be applied to intellectually disabled defendants.

The group called for a presumption, subject to challenge, that a person with an IQ below 75 should receive the exemption. It noted that Florida, one of the leading states for executions, adopted a strict IQ cutoff of 70, "even if all examining experts conclude, using the clinical definition, that the person is in fact intellectually disabled."

The committee also cited the case in Georgia of Warren Hill, who was sentenced to death for killing his cellmate. A court held that he had been shown to be disabled by a "preponderance of evidence" but not "beyond a reasonable doubt," as required by state rules that the panel called too stringent.

The state plan to proceed with Mr. Hill's execution has been delayed by a challenge to the state law that calls the source of execution drugs a "state secret."

The report said: "Lack of adequate counsel to represent capital defendants is likely the gravest of the problems that render the death penalty, as currently administered, arbitrary, unfair and fraught with serious error."

States including Alabama, Pennsylvania and Texas, it said, often compensate capital defense lawyers so poorly that a proper defense is "nearly impossible."

States should analyze data for signs of racial disparities in capital punishment, one of the concerns raised by President Obama, the report said.

The group recognized a dilemma in its call for the involvement of better-trained doctors and other medical technicians in the administering of lethal drugs. Most doctors and nurses abide by the American Medical Association's policy forbidding participation in executions.

But the risks of mistakes without well-trained personnel are so great, the panel said, that states should delay executions unless trained professionals are available.

A death penalty advocacy group, the Criminal Justice Legal Foundation, issued a statement criticizing the Constitution Project as one-sided and its report as failing to note that the main problem with capital punishment was that the appeals process delays it for far too long.

JOHN SCHWARTZ contributed reporting.

Nevada Execution Is Blocked After Drugmaker Sues

BY RICHARD A. OPPEL JR. | JULY 11, 2018

NEVADA'S EXECUTION OF a man convicted of murder was halted on Wednesday, after the manufacturer of one of the drugs that was to be used in the lethal injection argued that the state had obtained its product illicitly.

A district court judge issued a temporary restraining order preventing Nevada officials from using the drug in the execution. It was the first time that a pharmaceutical manufacturer has been able to stop an execution — at least temporarily. It is likely to intensify the battle between officials in death-penalty states and drugmakers that object to their products being used to kill inmates.

Nevada had planned to use three drugs in the execution of Scott Dozier, who has been on death row since 2007: one as a sedative, one to paralyze him, and the powerful synthetic opioid fentanyl to help kill him. The execution would have been the first to use fentanyl, which kills thousands of Americans every year and is at the forefront of the nation's overdose crisis.

The potential use of commonly abused narcotics like fentanyl in executions has alarmed human-rights organizations. They fear that prison officials in death-penalty states, facing objections from pharmaceutical companies, will turn to the black market to obtain those narcotics, bolstering trafficking networks at the same time authorities are desperately trying to curb them.

But the drug that led to the postponement of the execution on Wednesday was not fentanyl but midazolam, the sedative in the three-drug cocktail, whose use in executions has been bitterly disputed for different reasons. Judge Elizabeth Gonzalez of the Clark County District Court issued the restraining order.

Alvogen, the drug's manufacturer, had sued to block its use, saying Nevada obtained the drug under false pretenses because the company did not want it to be acquired for use in capital punishment. Alvogen said it would suffer "immediate and irreparable harm" if the medication were used for such purposes.

State officials bought the drug from a wholesale distributor, Cardinal Health, but did so without disclosing that it was to be used in an execution and not for a therapeutic purpose, according to Alvogen's lawyers.

The plaintiffs said Nevada officials had also instructed Cardinal Health to ship the drug to a state office in Las Vegas instead of to the state prison in Ely, Nev., more than 200 miles away, where the death chamber is. This was done, they said, "to further the implication that the midazolam was for a legitimate medical purpose."

Nevada had also planned to use a paralytic drug, cisatracurium besylate, whose maker, Sandoz, also tried to stop it from being used in the execution.

The state said it would not proceed with the execution Wednesday night if officials were not allowed to use midazolam. If Nevada were permanently prevented from using the medication, it would have to find another combination of drugs to execute Mr. Dozier.

Judge Gonzalez's ruling was hailed by human rights groups and anti-death penalty activists.

"This ruling affirms that the makers of medicines have a right to decide how their products are used," said Maya Foa, the director of Reprieve, a human-rights organization based in London. "These lawsuits exposed how Nevada ignored drug-safety laws designed to protect the public and used subterfuge to undermine private contracts."

In a statement issued after the ruling, the Nevada Department of Corrections said the execution "has been postponed."

Critics had warned that Mr. Dozier could endure a prolonged and excruciating death. The midazolam, they said, was likely not to render him fully unconscious, and when the fentanyl was injected, he would have to endure the sensation of suffocation. High doses of fentanyl kill by severely depressing the respiratory system.

The third drug to be injected — the paralytic agent — would have prevented Mr. Dozier from writhing on the gurney or showing any outward signs of pain, even as he suffered an agonizing death, the critics added. They argued that the paralytic could potentially mask the suffering involved in a botched execution. But Mr. Dozier said he was fine with all of that. He has waived appeals of his death sentence and told the judge in his case that he wanted to die, even if he suffered in the process.

In an interview this week with The Las Vegas Review-Journal, Mr. Dozier, 47, said his desire to be executed hadn't waned even after learning that the state intended to use an experimental drug protocol.

"Life in prison isn't a life," Mr. Dozier told the newspaper. "This isn't living, man. It's just surviving."

He added: "If people say they're going to kill me, get to it."

Fentanyl Used to Execute Nebraska Inmate, in a First for U.S.

BY MITCH SMITH | AUG. 14, 2018

LINCOLN, NEB. — Prison officials in Nebraska used the powerful opioid fentanyl to help execute a convicted murderer on Tuesday, the first such use of the drug in the United States and the first execution in the state since voters overturned a death penalty ban in 2016.

The use of fentanyl, an opioid at the heart of the nation's overdose crisis, as part of a previously untested four-drug cocktail drew concern from death penalty experts who questioned how the execution unfolded. And here in Nebraska, a state that last killed a prisoner in 1997, the lethal injection represented a stark political turnabout from when legislators outlawed capital punishment three years ago.

The condemned man, Carey Dean Moore, 60, had been convicted of killing two Omaha taxi drivers decades ago and did not seek a reprieve in his final months. He was pronounced dead at 10:47 a.m. at the Nebraska State Penitentiary, officials said, 23 minutes after the first drug was administered. Mr. Moore breathed heavily at one point and coughed, said four Nebraska journalists whom the state selected to watch the execution. Mr. Moore's face turned red, then purple.

The four-drug cocktail contained diazepam, a tranquilizer; fentanyl citrate, a powerful synthetic opioid that can block breathing and knock out consciousness; cisatracurium besylate, a muscle relaxant; and potassium chloride, which stops the heart.

This method could open a new avenue for states that have increasingly struggled to find execution drugs as suppliers have clamped down on how their products are used. But the unprecedented use of fentanyl in an execution chamber raised new questions, with death penalty observers warning that any untested method brought risks.

"Simply because people are dying as a result of fentanyl doesn't mean they're dying in a way that would be considered acceptable as

LUKE FRANKE FOR THE NEW YORK TIMES

The Nebraska State Penitentiary in Lincoln, Neb., where Carey Dean Moore was executed on Tuesday.

a form of execution," Deborah Denno, a law professor at Fordham University who has studied capital punishment, said in an interview before Mr. Moore's death.

Robert Dunham, the executive director of the nonprofit Death Penalty Information Center, said the journalists' accounts of the Nebraska execution left open the possibility that something went wrong.

"I can't tell from the description whether it's an indication of an execution gone bad or there are just question marks," said Mr. Dunham, who added that the execution took longer than the 15 or so minutes that he had anticipated. He said the descriptions of Mr. Moore coughing and his face reddening were concerning.

Scott Frakes, the state corrections director, who in the months before the execution refused to disclose the source of the drugs, spoke to reporters for roughly a minute after Mr. Moore died and did not answer questions.

"I am required to carry out the order of the court," Mr. Frakes said. "This agency has done so with professionalism, respect for the process and dignity for all involved."

Nebraska has a particularly complicated history with capital punishment. Before Tuesday, the state had not carried out an execution since 1997 and had never killed someone by lethal injection. (The state most recently had used an electric chair.)

A bipartisan mix of Nebraska legislators voted in 2015 to outlaw capital punishment, citing a mix of moral and financial reasons, and then overrode Gov. Pete Ricketts's veto. But Mr. Ricketts, a Republican, and his wealthy family bankrolled a ballot referendum that gave voters a chance to decide the issue. Nebraskans voted overwhelmingly in 2016 to reinstate the death penalty.

In recent weeks, the state's Roman Catholic bishops, citing a new teaching by Pope Francis that capital punishment is wrong in all cases, urged church members to contact state officials and try to block the execution. Mr. Ricketts is Catholic, but he said the pope's decision would not change his stance on Mr. Moore's execution.

"While I respect the pope's perspective, capital punishment remains the will of the people and the law of the state of Nebraska," Mr. Ricketts said in a statement earlier this month. "It is an important tool to protect our corrections officers and public safety. The state continues to carry out the sentences ordered by the court."

Mr. Ricketts's spokesman did not respond to requests for comment on Tuesday.

The Nebraska journalists who witnessed Mr. Moore's execution said it appeared to go as planned, though some parts of the process were conducted out of their view. Mr. Moore mouthed the words "I love you" to the witnesses he selected, the journalists said, and turned his head at various points in the execution process.

Mr. Moore, who robbed and killed Reuel Van Ness Jr. and Maynard Helgeland in a five-day crime spree in 1979, was among the longest-serving death row inmates in the country. Mr. Moore had seen

LUKE FRANKE FOR THE NEW YORK TIMES

A man prayed outside of the Nebraska State Penitentiary on Tuesday. Roman Catholic bishops had urged church members to contact state officials and try to block the execution.

previous execution dates come and go and had expressed frustration with the repeated delays. People close to him had said he was ready to die.

Still, his execution remained in question until his final hours. Two pharmaceutical companies tried to block the execution in federal court, claiming their reputations would suffer if the killing proceeded. And prison officials said Tuesday morning that they were consulting with the state attorney general to make sure no court issued a stay.

Outside the prison, a steady rain fell all morning as a small group of death penalty protesters gathered on the lawn. Several police officers and state troopers were posted in the area, but there were no obvious problems. The prison yard, alongside a major highway, appeared empty.

Eleven more men remain on Nebraska's death row, and prosecutors are seeking the death penalty in some pending cases. Still, it is unclear when and if the state will kill another inmate. The state's supply of one of the drugs used in the cocktail to kill Mr. Moore expires at the end of this month, and another expires in October.

Mr. Frakes, the Nebraska corrections director, said in a court filing this month that execution drugs "are difficult, if nearly impossible, to obtain," and that he has no replacement sources.

"A temporary restraining order or injunction," Mr. Frakes said in the court filing seeking to carry out Mr. Moore's execution, "would more than likely have the effect of changing Nebraska's final death sentence into a de facto sentence of life in prison for Carey Dean Moore."

Mr. Moore said little on Tuesday before the execution, according to the four reporters the state selected to witness the process. But he did write a page-long, handwritten letter acknowledging guilt and reiterating that he did not wish to fight the execution in court.

Mr. Moore wrote that he hoped lawyers would help his brother, who is on parole, and Nebraska death row inmates who claim they are innocent.

He signed the letter "Carey Dean Moore, ex-Death Row Inmate."

Glossary

abrogation Abolition through authoritative means.

adjudge To rule or decide judicially.

adjudication A judicial sentence.

amelioration Improvement or enhancement.

countenance To sanction or approve.

desideratum Something desirable or considered necessary.

divestiture The dispossession or disposal of authority.

dynamo A generator by which electrical energy is generated.

emulate To imitate or strive to match.

ex rel. Abbreviation of the legal term "ex relatione" used in the titles of legal proceedings to indicate the party on behalf of whom the state is acting.

exemplification A case or instance that serves as an example.

felonious Of or relating to a grave crime classified as a felony.

habeas corpus A writ questioning the legality of an individual's detainment in custody.

indigent Lacking financial means; suffering from poverty.

inimical Adverse or hostile.

jurisprudence A course or body of court decisions.

Lombroso, Cesare A 19th-century Italian criminologist known for his theory that criminal behavior was dictated by inherited genetic markers and, therefore, that potential criminals could be identified by physical traits.

majoritarianism The practice or principle of decision-making by majority.

pilfer To steal, especially in small amounts, yet repeatedly, so as to go unnoticed.

pusillanimous Lacking resolution; marked by hesitation or timidity.

regicide The murder of a royal.

restitution The legal act of repayment or an offering of an equivalent to compensate for injury.

soporific An agent intended to cause sleep or tending to dull awareness and alertness.

spurious Falsified or deceitful.

usurp To take or seize by force and without right.

writ of certiorari A written order issued by a superior court to review the records of an inferior court.

Media Literacy Terms

"Media literacy" refers to the ability to access, understand, critically assess and create media. The following terms are important components of media literacy, and they will help you critically engage with the articles in this title.

angle The aspect of a news story that a journalist focuses on and develops.

balance Principle of journalism that both perspectives of an argument should be presented in a fair way.

commentary A type of story that is an expression of opinion on recent events by a journalist generally known as a commentator.

credibility The quality of being trustworthy and believable, said of a journalistic source.

impartiality Principle of journalism that a story should not reflect a journalist's bias and should contain balance.

intention The motive or reason behind something, such as the publication of a news story.

interview story A type of story in which the facts are gathered primarily by interviewing another person or persons.

op-ed An opinion piece that reflects a prominent individual's opinion on a topic of interest.

reliability The quality of being dependable and accurate, said of a journalistic source.

tone A manner of expression in writing or speech.

Media Literacy Questions

1. What is the intention of the article "Is the Death Penalty an Actual Check to Crime?" (on page 11)? How does Dr. Spitzka support his argument? How effectively does the article achieve its intended purpose?

2. Does "Who Decides Who Will Die? Even Within States, It Varies" (on page 29) display the journalistic principle of balance?

3. What is Barbara Fitzgerald's angle in "Rethinking the Death Penalty" (on page 44)?

4. "California Ruling on Capital Punishment" (on page 58), "Why the Death Penalty Must Be Abolished" (on page 60) and "Legality of Death Penalty" (on page 61) are a series of letters to the editor published in early 1972. What is the intention of each of the three letters?

5. Compare the articles "Death Penalty Abolished in Bill" (on page 86) and "Too Young to Die?" (on page 109). What type of story is each article? Compare their headlines. What do you think is the intention of each headline?

6. In the article "Citing 'National Consensus,' Justices Bar Death Penalty for Retarded Defendants" (on page 93), Linda Greenhouse reports on a Supreme Court ruling. Published just a few days later, "Excerpts From Ruling and Dissent on Who Decides the Death Penalty" (on page 178) is a collection of quoted excerpts from another Supreme Court ruling. What are the strengths and weaknesses of each article's approach?

7. "Citing 'National Consensus,' Justices Bar Death Penalty for Retarded Defendants" (on page 93), "Supreme Court, 5-4, Forbids Execution in Juvenile Crime" (on page 126) and "Supreme Court Allows Lethal Injection for Execution" (on page 196) were all written by Linda Greenhouse. Identify similarities in Greenhouse's tone and writing style between articles.

8. What is Ron Rosenbaum's angle in "Too Young to Die?" (on page 109)? Why do you think he chose that angle? What effect do you think his approach is meant to achieve?

9. "Compassionate Capital Punishment" (on page 166) is an article written for a recurring column. What is the format of this piece? What do you think is the intention of the column it forms a part of?

10. The article "Cruel and Unusual History" (on page 192) is an example of an op-ed. Identify how Gilbert King's attitude and tone help convey his opinion on the topic.

11. Identify the sources in the article "Panel Urges One-Drug Lethal Injections" (on page 201)? How does Erik Eckholm attribute information to these sources?

Citations

All citations in this list are formatted according to the Modern Language Association's (MLA) style guide.

BOOK CITATION

THE NEW YORK TIMES EDITORIAL STAFF. *The Death Penalty*. New York: New York Times Educational Publishing, 2020.

ONLINE ARTICLE CITATIONS

ALTMAN, LAWRENCE K. "Focus on Doctors and Executions." *The New York Times*, 20 Mar. 1994, https://www.nytimes.com/1994/03/20/us/focus-on-doctors-and-executions.html.

ECKHOLM, ERIK. "Panel Urges One-Drug Lethal Injections." *The New York Times*, 7 May 2014, https://www.nytimes.com/2014/05/07/us/panel-urges-one-drug-lethal-injections.html.

ECKHOLM, ERIK. "Studies Find Death Penalty Tied to Race of the Victims." *The New York Times*, 24 Feb. 1995, https://www.nytimes.com/1995/02/24/nyregion/studies-find-death-penalty-tied-to-race-of-the-victims.html.

FESSENDEN, FORD. "Deadly Statistics: A Survey of Crime and Punishment." *The New York Times*, 22 Sept. 2000, https://www.nytimes.com/2000/09/22/us/deadly-statistics-a-survey-of-crime-and-punishment.html.

FISKE, EDWARD B. "Lutherans Hit Death Penalty: Aides of 3.3 Million-Member Church Favor a Ban." *The New York Times*, 30 June 1966, https://www.nytimes.com/2018/08/02/world/europe/pope-death-penalty.html.

FITZGERALD, BARBARA. "Rethinking the Death Penalty." *The New York Times*, 14 Dec. 2003, https://www.nytimes.com/2003/12/14/nyregion/rethinking-the-death-penalty.html.

FLINT, AUSTIN, DR. "The Penalty of Death." *The New York Times*, 7 Aug. 1898, https://www.nytimes.com/1898/08/07/archives/the-penalty-of-death.html.

GOLDBERG, ARTHUR J., AND ALAN M. DERSHOWITZ. "An End to the Death Penalty." *The New York Times*, 6 June 1971, https://www.nytimes.com/1971/06/06/archives/an-end-to-the-death-penalty.html.

GRADY, DENISE. "Doctors See Way to Cut Suffering in Executions." *The New York Times*, 23 June 2006, https://www.nytimes.com/2006/06/23/us/23inject.html.

GRAHAM, FRED P. "Court Spares 600." *The New York Times*, 30 June 1972, https://www.nytimes.com/1972/06/30/archives/court-spares-600-4-justices-named-by-nixon-all-dissent-in-historic.html.

GREENHOUSE, LINDA. "Citing 'National Consensus,' Justices Bar Death Penalty for Retarded Defendants." *The New York Times*, 21 June 2002, https://www.nytimes.com/2002/06/21/us/supreme-court-death-penalty-citing-national-consensus-justices-bar-death-penalty.html.

GREENHOUSE, LINDA. "Supreme Court Allows Lethal Injection for Execution." *The New York Times*, 17 Apr. 2008, https://www.nytimes.com/2008/04/17/us/16cnd-scotus.html.

GREENHOUSE, LINDA. "Supreme Court, 5-4, Forbids Execution in Juvenile Crime." *The New York Times*, 2 Mar. 2005, https://www.nytimes.com/2005/03/02/politics/supreme-court-54-forbids-execution-in-juvenile-crime.html.

JOHNSON, KIRK. "Washington State Supreme Court Deems Death Penalty Unconstitutional." *The New York Times*, 11 Oct. 2018, https://www.nytimes.com/2018/10/11/us/death-penalty-ruling-washington-state.html.

KING, GILBERT. "Cruel and Unusual History." *The New York Times*, 23 Apr. 2008, https://www.nytimes.com/2008/04/23/opinion/23king.html.

KLOSTERMAN, CHUCK. "Compassionate Capital Punishment." *The New York Times*, 8 Aug. 2014, https://www.nytimes.com/2014/08/10/magazine/compassionate-capital-punishment.html.

KNEELAND, DOUGLAS. "Backers of the Death Penalty Are Making Scant Progress." *The New York Times*, 9 May 1977, https://www.nytimes.com/1977/05/09/archives/backers-of-the-death-penalty-are-making-scant-progress-backers-of.html.

LEWIN, TAMAR. "Who Decides Who Will Die? Even Within States, It Varies." *The New York Times*, 23 Feb. 1995, https://www.nytimes.com/1995/02/23/us/who-decides-who-will-die-even-within-states-it-varies.html.

LIPTAK, ADAM. "Court Extends Curb on the Death Penalty in a Florida Ruling." *The New York Times*, 27 May 2014, https://www.nytimes.com/2014/05/28/us/court-rules-against-florida-iq-rule-in-death-cases.html.

THE NEW YORK TIMES. "Blackmun: 'I … Concede That the Death Penalty Experiment Has Failed.' " *The New York Times*, 23 Feb. 1994, https://www.nytimes.com/1994/02/23/us/blackmun-i-concede-that-the-death-penalty-experiment-has-failed.html.

THE NEW YORK TIMES. "California Ruling on Capital Punishment." *The New York Times*, 27 Feb. 1972, https://www.nytimes.com/1972/02/27/archives/california-ruling-on-capital-punishment.html.

THE NEW YORK TIMES. "Casting Off a Remnant of Racism." *The New York Times*, 10 July 1977, https://www.nytimes.com/1977/07/10/archives/casting-off-a-remnant-of-racism.html.

THE NEW YORK TIMES. "The Death Penalty." *The New York Times*, 3 Mar. 1910, https://www.nytimes.com/1910/03/03/archives/the-death-penalty.html.

THE NEW YORK TIMES. "Death Penalty Abolished in Bill." *The New York Times*, 7 Apr. 1914, https://www.nytimes.com/1914/04/07/archives/death-penalty-abolished-in-bill-whitman-asks-gov-glynn-for-hearing.html.

THE NEW YORK TIMES. "Excerpts From Ruling and Dissent on Who Decides the Death Penalty." *The New York Times*, 25 June 2002, https://www.nytimes.com/2002/06/25/us/supreme-court-excerpts-ruling-dissent-who-decides-death-penalty.html.

THE NEW YORK TIMES. "Florida's Unconstitutional Death Penalty." *The New York Times*, 3 Mar. 2014, https://www.nytimes.com/2014/03/04/opinion/floridas-unconstitutional-death-penalty.html.

THE NEW YORK TIMES. "Is the Death Penalty an Actual Check to Crime?" *The New York Times*, 16 May 1909, https://www.nytimes.com/1909/05/16/archives/is the-death-penalty-an-actual-check-to-crime-dr-edward-c-spitzka.html.

THE NEW YORK TIMES. "The Kemmler Execution: Dr. C. E. Spitzka Tells Doctors and Lawyers All About It." *The New York Times*, 11 Nov. 1890, https://www.nytimes.com/1890/11/11/archives/the-kemmler-execution-dr-ce-spitzka-tells-doctors-and-lawyers-all-a.html.

THE NEW YORK TIMES. "Last Chance for Warren Hill." *The New York Times*, 11 July 2013, https://www.nytimes.com/2013/07/12/opinion/last-chance-for-warren-hill.html.

THE NEW YORK TIMES. "Legality of Death Penalty." *The New York Times*, 2 Apr. 1972, https://www.nytimes.com/1972/04/02/archives/legality-of-death-penalty.html.

THE NEW YORK TIMES. "Panel Urges End to Death Penalty: Psychiatrists Told That It Fails as a Deterrent." *The New York Times*, 15 May, 1966. https://

www.nytimes.com/1966/05/15/archives/panel-urges-end-to-death-penalty-psychiatrists-told-that-it-fails-a.html.

THE NEW YORK TIMES. "Reform Jews Ask Death Penalty End." *The New York Times*, 26 Apr. 1959, https://www.nytimes.com/1959/04/26/archives/reform-jews-ask-death-penalty-end.html.

THE NEW YORK TIMES. "Scalia: Fifth Amendment 'Clearly Permits the Death Penalty.' " *The New York Times*, 23 Feb. 1994, https://www.nytimes.com/1994/02/23/us/scalia-fifth-amendment-clearly-permits-the-death-penalty.html.

THE NEW YORK TIMES. "Why the Death Penalty Must Be Abolished." *The New York Times*, 12 Mar. 1972, https://www.nytimes.com/1972/03/12/archives/why-the-death-penalty-must-be-abolished.html.

NOBLE, KENNETH B. "High Court to Decide Whether Death Penalty Discriminates Against Blacks." *The New York Times*, 23 Mar. 1987, https://www.nytimes.com/1987/03/23/us/high-court-to-decide-whether-death-penalty-discriminates-against-blacks.html.

OELSNER, LESLEY. "Court to Review Death Penalty Issue." *The New York Times*, 23 Jan. 1976, https://www.nytimes.com/1976/01/23/archives/court-to-review-death-penalty-issue.html.

OPPEL, RICHARD A., JR. "Nevada Execution Is Blocked After Drugmaker Sues." *The New York Times*, 11 July 2018, https://www.nytimes.com/2018/07/11/us/dozier-execution-fentanyl.html.

POVOLEDO, ELISABETTA, AND LAURIE GOODSTEIN. "Pope Francis Declares Death Penalty Unacceptable in All Cases." *The New York Times*, 2 Aug. 2018, https://www.nytimes.com/2018/08/02/world/europe/pope-death-penalty.html.

REINHOLD, ROBERT. "Technician Executes Murderer in Texas by Lethal Injection." *The New York Times*, 7 Dec. 1982, https://www.nytimes.com/1982/12/07/us/technician-executes-murderer-in-texas-by-lethal-injection.html.

ROSENBAUM, RON. "Too Young to Die?" *The New York Times*, 12 Mar. 1989, https://www.nytimes.com/1989/03/12/magazine/too-young-to-die.html.

RUSSO, JOHN F. "Death Penalty Is Favored." *The New York Times*, 8 Aug. 1976, https://www.nytimes.com/1976/08/08/archives/new-jersey-weekly-death-penalty-is-favored.html.

SMITH, MITCH. "Fentanyl Used to Execute Nebraska Inmate, in a First for U.S." *The New York Times*, 14 Aug. 2018, https://www.nytimes.com/2018/08/14/us/carey-dean-moore-nebraska-execution-fentanyl.html.

STEINFELS, PETER. "Milestone in Death Penalty Fight, but Still a Way to Go."

The New York Times, 22 Dec. 2007, https://www.nytimes.com/2007/12/22/us/22beliefs.html.

TAYLOR, STUART, JR. "Constitution Sometimes Prohibits Executing the Insane, Justices Say." *The New York Times*, 27 June 1986, https://www.nytimes.com/1986/06/27/us/constitution-sometimes-prohibits-executing-the-insane-justices-say.html.

WEAVER, WARREN, JR. "Death Penalty a 300-Year Issue in America." *The New York Times*, 3 July 1976, https://www.nytimes.com/1976/07/03/archives/death-penalty-a-300year-issue-in-america.html.

WICKER, TOM. "Death Again in California." *The New York Times*, 12 Nov. 1972, https://www.nytimes.com/1972/11/12/archives/death-again-in-california.html.

WOOD, LEWIS. "Boy, 17, Will Face Second Execution." *The New York Times*, 14 Jan. 1947, https://www.nytimes.com/1947/01/14/archives/boy-17-will-face-second-execution-supreme-court-rules-5-to-4.html.

Index

This book is current up until the time of printing. For the most up-to-date reporting, visit www.nytimes.com.